Jack stared at his reflection critically, rubbing a hand over his stubbled jaw. The hours of travelling had left him tired, dishevelled and desperately in need of a shave.

It was not the face of a father.

But he was going to be one, whether his marriage survived or not.

They'd been discussing separation, divorce, before he'd left. Not parenthood. How had she felt when she'd discovered she was pregnant? Shocked? Or secretly pleased?

One thing was for sure—if he couldn't trust Liz, he would lose her.

Lose *them*.

He looked down at his hand as he remembered the solid push he'd felt from Liz's stomach... from the baby. His baby.

His stomach swooped in another quick dive. He was going to be a *father*.

Born in New Zealand, **Sharon Archer** now lives in county Victoria, Australia, with her husband Glenn, one lame horse and five pensionable hens. Always an avid reader, she discovered Mills & Boon as a teenager through Lucy Walker's fabulous Outback Australia stories. Now she lives in a gorgeous bush setting, and loves the native fauna that visits regularly... Well, maybe not the possum which coughs outside the bedroom window in the middle of the night.

The move to acreage brought a keen interest in bushfire management (she runs the fireguard group in her area) as well as free time to dabble in woodwork, genealogy (her advice is...don't get her started!), horse-riding and motorcycling—as a pillion or in charge of the handlebars.

Free time turned into words on paper! And the dream to be a writer gathered momentum. With her background in a medical laboratory, what better line to write for than Mills & Boon® Medical™ Romance?

Recent titles by the same author:

SINGLE FATHER: WIFE AND MOTHER WANTED

MARRIAGE REUNITED: BABY ON THE WAY

BY
SHARON ARCHER

MILLS & BOON

First published in Great Britain 2009
Harlequin Mills & Boon Limited
Eton House, 18-24 Paradis

© Sharon Archer 2009

ISBN: 978 0 263 20836 8

Set in Times Roman 10½ on 12 pt
07-0809-51641

Harlequin Mills & Boon policy is to use papers that are natural, renewable and recyclable products and made from wood grown in sustainable forests. The logging and manufacturing process conform to the legal environmental regulations of the country of origin.

Printed and bound in Great Britain
by CPI Antony Rowe, Chippenham, Wiltshire

MARRIAGE REUNITED: BABY ON THE WAY

I'd like to especially thank my editor,
Lucy Gilmour, for her suggestions, encouragement
and belief in my manuscripts.

Thank you always to Anna Campbell, Rachel Bailey
and Marion Lennox. You are the best!

Thank you, too, to Judy Griffiths and Serena Tatti
for your input on this book.

And especially thanks to my husband, Glenn,
for his unstinting support with everything!

CHAPTER ONE

JACK CAMPBELL slipped into the hospital room and closed the door. Muted sounds of the emergency department filtered through to him, the jingle of an instrument trolley, the squeak of a rubber-soled shoe.

The pungent smell of antiseptic. A decades-old aversion leaped across the years to roll nausea through his stomach. For a split second, he was thirteen years old again—wretched, angry, useless—listening to nurses discuss the rapidly failing infant that had just come in. His sister, his family.

He blew out a breath, made a conscious effort to push down the unwelcome, unhelpful recollection.

He was here to see Liz.

Dr Elizabeth Campbell…his wife… He clenched his jaw. Soon-to-be ex-wife if she had anything to do with it.

She lay on a gurney, her back towards him. A grey blanket skimmed the curves of her shoulder and hip. Dark curls tumbled across a small, flat pillow. His fingers curled involuntarily with the memory of the silky strands slipping across his skin. They had a lot of talking, a lot of healing to do before he could look forward to that intimacy.

A louder clatter came from outside the door. So used to the background noise of the hospital, Liz still didn't wake, didn't even stir. She always slept serenely, such a contrast to the snapping vitality she radiated when she was awake.

The duty nurse said Liz had been up for most of the night treating the victims of a nasty car accident.

He suddenly realised the nurse's welcome had been much warmer than he deserved. Hadn't Liz told her colleagues that her marriage—*their* marriage—was on shaky ground? His spirits lifted briefly, then plunged as he wondered if the state of their relationship was simply an insignificant detail to her, not worth mentioning.

He leaned back against the door and ran a tired hand over his face. Whiskers scraped his palm, reminding him that he should have showered and shaved at the airport after the long flight from the States. Instead, he'd hired a car and driven more hours to be here.

To see the woman who slept so soundly just a few steps away.

So why was he delaying the moment of confrontation?

Dread spasmed in his gut. Because he didn't know how she was going to handle his return. Now that he was here, his five months away with minimal communication felt unreasonable—even given their mutual separation. Stilted phone calls, always with the unspoken knowledge that once their marriage was dissolved, they had no claim on each other.

How would she take the decisions he'd made without consulting her? Accepting the position of captain in Dustin's fire brigade.

Not giving her the easy divorce he'd promised before he'd left.

Somewhere in the last few months of battling fires in California, he'd realised how important Liz was to him. What a fool he'd been to think it would be easy to move on.

He'd even come to the conclusion he could handle discussing parenthood. He tried to imagine Liz heavy with pregnancy—and failed. Tried to picture himself holding a baby—and an icy chill speared out of his heart. He swallowed hard. All he had to do was overcome that instinctive rejection. That was *all*.

He wanted to fight for his marriage, to tackle their problems. And when they were done, if she still wanted him out of her life, then he'd go.

He touched the pocket that held two open airline tickets to New Zealand. Tickets to the place they'd begun their marriage. Tickets to paradise. An inspiration…or a crazy idea born of desperation.

Squaring his shoulders, he pushed away from the door. Long strides took him to the gurney.

He reached out to touch Liz, his hand hovering over her shoulder before slowly dropping to his side. His eyes lingered on her profile, the curve of her cheek, eyelashes curled in smudgy purple shadows that spoke of tiredness. She took on so much responsibility, worked too hard. But there was no telling her to slow down. A bitter-sweet longing pierced his heart to see her looking so young and vulnerable.

On impulse, he leaned down and pressed his lips to her cheek just in front of her ear. Her skin was warm and soft. She sighed. He inhaled the heady fragrance of the woman he loved, intended to love for the rest of his life. If he could find a way to turn things around, if he could find a way to overcome his fear. He had to believe it was possible.

She rolled slightly, reaching up to hook a hand around his neck. Her fingers threaded through his hair, tugging his head closer as she offered him her mouth.

He wrestled with his conscience. Her invitation was hard to resist. But she still seemed half-asleep, which was unusual since she was used to waking instantly. 'Liz?'

'Jack,' she murmured, her hand stroking across the nape of his neck.

His heart swelled. She knew who he was. He stopped questioning, touched his mouth to hers, sinking into the welcome taste and texture. He was home.

* * *

Lips moved on hers. The wonderful, clever, knowing lips of her husband, her lover. At once familiar and unbelievably exciting, flooding her body with sensual need. Kissing her, nibbling and rubbing sensitive nerve endings to life. The familiar feel, a haven conjured up by a dream.

She parted her lips in invitation, wanting more and after a moment the light kiss became more demanding, firm and masterful. The taste of him, the feel of him, so infinitely beloved. Something she never wanted to lose. The thought brought a lump of emotion to her throat. Hot tears pushed at her eyelids before seeping out to trickle down her temple into her ears.

The lips drifted away to work their magic along her jaw.

'Jack.'

Arching slightly, she gave him access to her throat and the delicious caress was instantly there to please her. Bliss. She ached for his touch everywhere.

Stubble rasped across her chin as he moved back to her mouth, a mixture of pleasure and discomfort. Why couldn't she have dreamed him up after he'd shaved? She tried to push the fretful thought away, not wanting to spoil the precious moment.

'Liz,' groaned her dream lover. Her eyes flew open as the word smashed away the last vestiges of sleep.

'What the—? Jack!' The rhythm of her heart bounded, painful and erratic with panic. She sat up abruptly, her head connecting with something hard.

'Hell, Liz!' The muffled protest behind her registered as she swung her feet to the floor and stood up. She put a hand on the gurney's metal frame and gulped down the slide of queasiness crawling up her throat.

Steadier, she took a deep breath and folded her arms protectively across her body. She turned slowly to stare at the man on the other side of the narrow mattress.

'Just what do you think you're doing?' She'd meant the

words to come out strong, determined. Outraged. Instead, she sounded almost husky, breathless.

Jack's hand stopped moving his lower jaw and fell to his side. The room seemed to lurch again as he gave her a lopsided smile.

'Kissing my wife?' The sexy voice stroked along her auditory nerves. So much more potent when he was in the room with her than on the other end of a phone line.

She scowled as his answer drew her attention to his mouth. The gorgeous shape with its full bottom lip still tilted up at one corner. In her semi-conscious state, her lips had recognised him, welcomed his much-loved caress, responded to him. And if she was honest, she'd known on some level that her dream was too good, too real. But in the ultimate self-betrayal, she'd resisted the push to full awareness.

'I'm not your wife.' Her lips felt swollen, tremulous. Her traitorous body still hummed with the need his kiss had created.

'Yeah, you are.'

Muscles tightened around her chest. She wasn't prepared for this scene. 'Technically, yes. In reality, no.'

'Technically is what we've got, babe.' He watched her through narrowed eyes as though trying to gauge the emotion underlying her negative response. 'And what we have to talk about.'

'We did all our talking before you left.' She frowned at him. 'And don't call me babe.'

Why did he have to look so damned good? Big and rugged and fit. Tussled spikes of dark hair above a lean, angular face. She had to remember that underneath the stunning exterior he was cold, contained.

Untouchable. Her vulnerable heart squeezed. Common sense hadn't stopped her from falling for a man just like her distant, unresponsive father.

She and Jack were separated. Had agreed on it before he'd gone on secondment to the States. His months away fighting summer wildfires had given her a chance to get used to him not being around. There was no going back. She couldn't. Too much was at stake now.

She wasn't going to settle for a half-life, the way her mother had. Two years was more than enough time to invest in a mistake.

Of course, the marriage wasn't their only mistake.

She buttoned her lab coat, carefully holding the fabric away from her body. Thank goodness for the large, shapeless garment. And the light in here was fairly subdued. If she could just get out of the room…

'You can't just walk away from me, Liz. I'm not going anywhere until we've worked this through.'

'Please yourself.' With shaking fingers, she looped the stethoscope around her neck then stuffed her fists into the large coat pockets. 'Unlike you, I have work to do.'

She wasn't being fair to him. He'd been away, risking his life. But fair didn't matter right now.

Escape! That was all that mattered. Making a show of checking her watch, she went to walk past him.

At the last moment, he moved to stop her. Dumb luck had his hand land on the one thing she didn't want to discuss with him right now. She froze as an energetic thud bounced out of her abdomen to greet his touch.

His mouth dropped open as he snatched his hand away and looked down at her distended belly. She could still feel the imprint of his fingers through the heavy fabric of the coat.

'You're…' His eyes, dark blue and stunned, blinked back up to meet hers. He was so close that, despite the dimness, she could see the shock in the sudden pallor of his face. 'You're pregnant.'

'Yes.' She watched creases form at the edges of his eyes, could almost see the cogs turning over in his mind.

Was he doing the arithmetic? Their last attempt at talking about reconciliation had been a doozey. And she'd been in-cubating the results of their *discussion* for nearly six months now.

'Is it mine?'

Pain washed over her, snatching the breath from her lungs. Such cruelty from the mouth that had just kissed her so sweetly, so lovingly.

'Charming, Jack,' she said, squaring her shoulders and refusing to let him see how much he'd hurt her. 'Are you judging me by your own behaviour?'

She pushed past him and walked towards the door on rubbery knees. She hated scenes, but for five months she'd known this one was unavoidable.

'Liz!'

She blinked blurriness out of her vision and kept walking. Whatever he had to say could wait. But Jack was too quick for her. His hand on her arm stopped her before she could reach the door.

'I'm sorry.'

Her jaw dropped at the gruff words. An apology. That was new. She looked up at him.

'Yes, well…I am sorry. That was out of line.' He released her to run his hand through his hair, leaving tufts standing in its wake. His eyes, when they met hers, were wary. She could see his mouth working as though he was having trouble speaking, forming words. 'That last time we…?' The partial sentence was little more than a croak.

'I would think so, yes.'

'So you're about five months along?'

'Closer to six, actually.' She stroked a protective hand over her stomach. Given the bizarre gymnastics the rest of her system was doing at the moment, she was vaguely surprised that her womb wasn't being used for somersault practice. Couldn't the baby sense her mother's distress? Or perhaps that's why she was so still.

Jack's eyes followed the movement of her hand, a dazed look on his face. 'We're going to be parents in, what, three months?' His throat moved in a convulsive swallow. 'Twelve weeks?'

Her heart swooped, a dozen answers trembling on her tongue. But the last thing she wanted right now was to prolong this discussion. Liz settled for a simple, 'Close enough.' They could argue the semantics of parenthood another time.

'We've got more to talk about than I'd realised.' His eyes held a solemn appeal when they met hers.

'Perhaps, but not now.' She hardened her heart against the treacherous impulse to believe he could change. He'd just been caught off guard, his apology was evidence of how much. 'I really do have work to do. Are you...? Where are you...?' The words dried up on her tongue.

'Staying?' An eyebrow quirked as his dark eyes watched her quizzically. 'At home. Unless there's a reason why I shouldn't.'

'No. I...suppose it'll be okay...for a while... It's just that...' She trailed off again. She couldn't go back to the peculiar segregated life they'd been living before. Sharing a house, but not themselves. A half-life masquerading as a marriage. She'd used long hours at work to escape the house before Jack had gone overseas. That wasn't an option these days because she was too tired.

'Damn, Liz... What do you think I'm going to do?' He grimaced, his eyes shuttered. She was left with the fleeting impression that she'd hurt him. 'I'm still house-trained.' His lopsided smile was meant to disarm. 'And I haven't jumped on an unwilling woman for at least a month. Let alone one who's *pregnant* and unwilling.'

Did that mean he *had* jumped on a *willing* woman while he was away? She lifted her chin in rejection of the picture his words conjured up. What did it matter to her if he had been with someone? Once they were divorced, he could be with any damned woman he fancied.

She wanted a divorce…didn't she?

Suddenly, hot moisture burned beneath her eyelids, threatened to spill over. Bending her head for a few moments, she pulled at the wrinkled front of her coat as though straightening it was the most important thing in her life.

She heard him take a deep breath.

'Look, Liz, I'm tired. Can we have this discussion later, too? I'll use the spare bed if it'll make you happier.'

'I'm using it.' Her voice sounded hoarse with the ache in her throat.

'I see.' He looked away and she could see a muscle twitching along his jaw.

'It's the only bed made up so use it. I haven't been home to sleep in it since I changed the sheets yesterday.' As soon as the words were out she wished she could take them back. His eyes held hers for a long moment. She tensed, waiting for a derisive comment.

'Thanks,' he said.

She nodded briefly. On muscles wobbly with relief, she turned towards the door.

'Liz?'

She looked back at him.

'Could I borrow your keys, please?'

'My keys? Haven't you got yours?'

'The airline lost my luggage in California. I didn't want to risk missing my connecting flight home while someone tracked it down.'

He sounded exhausted, almost defeated, and she realised for the first time that there were dark circles under his eyes. Her heart ached with sympathy she didn't want to feel.

'Mine are in my locker, but there's a front-door key in the old pot-belly on the veranda.' She shrugged slightly at the patent surprise on his face. 'Pregnancy seems to have scrambled the thought processes that keep track of my keys. After

I locked myself out of the house a couple of times, I put a spare set outside.'

He regarded her in silence. 'Have you…been okay otherwise?'

'Mostly.' His question touched her to the core. He sounded like he cared. Foolish, foolish woman to let herself be affected by a few kind words. She forced her lips into a smile. No way was she going to tell him about the weeks of morning sickness when she'd wanted to curl up in a ball and have someone care for her. The days when she'd had to drag herself out of bed to come to work. Or the times she'd desperately needed a hug— his hug. 'Can you make sure you put the key back, please?'

'Sure.'

'Well…I'll see you later, then.'

Jack pulled into the driveway, a mantle of lethargy settling on his shoulders as he switched off the ignition of the rental car. He sat for a minute or two, noting the overgrown garden, the bush-covered hills of the Victorian high country that formed a familiar backdrop.

A mower droned soporifically in the distance. The sound of a dog barking in the neighbour's yard snapped him out of a daze. If he didn't move soon, he'd fall asleep right here.

Coming back had been the right thing. *More right than he'd realised when he'd made the decision.* Living in Dustin was the closest he'd come to having roots. The town was large enough to provide great services, small enough to be a real community. A great place to raise a family.

A lead weight dropped through his gut.

A family. Oh, God. He wasn't ready, he'd never be ready. A thin film of perspiration popped out of his pores, chilling his forehead and upper lip. He recognised his body's fight-or-flight response. Pointless trying to deal with this when he was punchy with jet-lag.

Grabbing his carry-on bag, he forced his tired legs up the veranda steps. He scrupulously returned the key to the old pot belly stove after he'd used it. Inside the house, he tapped the door with his heel, listening to the latch snick behind him as he let the familiar smells soak in. Delicate, delicious scents with tones of lavender and fresh pine cones. And a trace of Liz's favourite soap.

This house and Liz were home, where he belonged, where he wanted to stay. He rubbed his sternum as he took inventory of the wide central hallway and the living areas off to each side. His heart felt too big for his chest. The months away had given him a poignant appreciation of things he'd taken for granted. The colours, soft, welcoming terracotta and greens, had been Liz's choice. He'd provided the brawn for the preparation and painting. And they'd both chosen the eclectic collection of new and second-hand furniture. Everything had been picked for comfort and appeal, not because it matched another item.

Liz had joked that she was exorcising the polished, regimented perfection of her childhood. If only all demons could be so easily disposed of. Not that he had a problem with his past. He'd simply used it as a blueprint of what to avoid. Growing up as the son of a drug addict had left him utterly clear about one aspect of his life. No dabbling, no social indulging. No chemical crutches needed to get him through each day. Not for any reason.

Not ever.

He tossed his car keys on the small hall desk and walked slowly through the house, pausing again in the doorway of the main bedroom. A vivid vision of Liz tumbled across the queen-sized mattress beneath his weight had heat scorching to his groin. He blinked the memory away.

Now the luxurious brocade spread hid the fact that the bed it covered was stripped and unused. A façade.

Like their marriage? His heart kicked painfully.

Not if he could help it.

He strode through to the spare room and dumped his carry-on bag onto the bed's pristine quilt cover. His mouth tightened.

Fresh sheets. The small domestic detail epitomised their estrangement. That and the question about where he was staying. Realistically, he hadn't expected to leap back into bed with her. But since when did they need fresh sheets between them?

Perhaps this was Liz's way of distancing herself from him even further. Things had been bad when he'd left, but at least they'd shared a bed right up until the final few weeks.

Or had they? Both their jobs meant nights away. He'd volunteered to do more than his fair share at the fire station. With a sinking feeling, he realised that Liz had probably been doing the same thing at the hospital.

He smiled grimly as he stripped off his shirt. The crackle of the airline tickets seemed to mock him. A second honeymoon to rekindle their relationship seemed laughably simplistic in the face of Liz's pregnancy. He threw his clothes on the chair in the corner before padding naked across the hall to the bathroom.

Leaning on the vanity unit, he stared at his reflection critically, rubbing a hand over his stubbled jaw. The hours of travelling had left him tired, dishevelled and desperately in need of a shave.

It was not the face of a father.

But he was going to be one, whether his marriage survived or not. A cold thrill swept over him, part dread, part some other emotion he didn't recognise.

Poor Liz. They'd been discussing separation, divorce before he'd left. Not parenthood. How had she felt when she discovered she was pregnant? Shocked? Or secretly pleased? She'd been off the Pill, but they'd used protection…though obviously not enough. He grinned wryly.

His smile faded as he remembered the spasm of hurt, quickly hidden, that had flashed across her face when he'd asked if the child was his. The question had risen from some deep, fortressed corner of his soul and emerged before he could think better of it.

'You really are a prize bastard, Campbell.' His voice sounded croaky, unnaturally loud in the silent house. He blew out a long breath. Liz didn't deserve to be measured by the women in his past. She wasn't the sort to betray him with another man. Cerebrally, he knew that…but how did he turn that into a gut-level, instinctive trust? One thing was for sure—if he couldn't, he would lose her.

Lose *them*.

He looked down at his hand, curled his fingers over the palm as he remembered the solid push he'd felt from Liz's stomach…from the baby. His baby.

He was going to be a *father*. His stomach swooped in another quick dive.

Hell, what did he know about family?

CHAPTER TWO

SIX hours later, rested and showered, Jack stood at the ward desk. On the other side, Liz leaned forward, her hands braced on either side of a stack of patient records.

'I'm working. I can't just leave.' Each word was enunciated with a frigid clarity that should have blistered his ears.

'Yes, you can.' For the first time he began to appreciate just how difficult the task he'd set himself was going to be. He took a slow deep breath. 'I've spoken to Tony Costello—'

'What? You've spoken to my boss?' Her voice was still pitched low in deference to the patients in the ward, but her intensity rammed into him. 'How dare you?'

'Easily.' He'd come too far to back down now. 'You're not to darken the hospital doors before tomorrow.'

If she had any idea of the scope of the discussions with Tony she'd be even angrier. He'd cross that bridge when he had to. Leaning on the counter, he willed his body to relax. The smile he forced to his mouth felt stiff with tension.

'I've got things to do.' Liz wore a hunted look as her eyes slid away from him to a pile of neatly stacked patient notes.

'Yes, you sure do. You have to come home with me.'

Her gaze, dark and revealing, darted back to his. She was afraid. *Of him?* The notion punched his breath away. His Liz was fearless. Surely, he was mistaken.

'Do I have to throw you over my shoulder, darlin'?' He was relieved there was no trace of his turmoil in his voice.

'In case you haven't noticed, I don't bend that way any more,' she grated out. Any hint of fear was burned away as her eyes glowed gold with anger.

He allowed his gaze to drift down to the mound of her abdomen. His chest tightened in an unexpected rush of possessiveness. His woman. His baby. 'No, I guess not. Okay, fireman's lift is out. How about I sweep you up and carry you out in my arms? Should cause quite a stir.'

'You wouldn't.' She scowled, pulling the edges of her white coat over her stomach and folding her arms.

'Try me.'

He held her gaze for a long moment before she huffed out a breath and looked down at the desk, her lips clamped in a firm line. A pang of sympathy tweaked at his conscience. She was no match for him now that he'd had a solid five hours sleep.

Since he'd been up, he'd returned the rental car to the depot and shopped for groceries. On the back seat of Liz's car sat half a dozen bags of necessities to stock the woefully depleted refrigerator he'd found at the house, at their home. He straightened, flexing his shoulders. Pregnant women needed to look after themselves. Or be looked after.

'Very well.' She straightened a pile of forms. 'But I need to check on one of the patients before I go. So you'll just have to wait.'

'Don't be long, sweetheart, or I'll come and find you,' he said softly as she rounded the desk to move past him.

The look she flashed him should have fried him on the spot. 'I'll be as long as I need to be.'

As he watched her moving down the corridor, her steps slower than normal, he knew he was doing the right thing whether she liked it or not. A peculiar mixture of emotions—

exasperation, love, and maybe just a touch of anger?—churned in his gut as she disappeared into one of the rooms.

He expelled a long sigh. They'd had so many arguments about starting a family in the six months before he'd gone overseas. He'd finally faced the fact that he didn't want to be a father. That the remnants of his paternal instinct had died more than a decade ago.

With Kylie's betrayal. *Kylie.* He hadn't thought about his teenage crush for years. The girl who'd told him he was going to be a father—only to dump him when she miscarried. And dump him hard, trashing his love and his fervent promises of marriage, support, fidelity. Even stripping him of his right to grieve for the lost baby with her confession that it wasn't his.

Perhaps his past wasn't as buried as he believed.

He rubbed a hand over his face and thought back to his last confrontation with Liz, on the day before he'd left. It'd been very cold, very civilised after the preceding months of hot words and hotter, hope-filled reconciliations.

But regardless of the physical passion that flared between them, he hadn't been able to overcome the obstacle of Liz's desire to have a family. His argument, that they had something special and didn't need children to complete their relationship, hadn't swayed her at all. He'd agreed to give Liz a divorce. He smiled grimly. Looking at it from Liz's perspective, though, she'd been unable to overcome his entrenched resistance to becoming a father.

Stalemate.

Not that it mattered now. A moment's careless pleasure and they were going to be parents. Though, in fairness to both of them, they hadn't been careless, just unlucky. Their usual contraceptive regimen had failed.

Or *had* Liz been deliberately careless? The muscles of his scalp contracted, pulling at his already tense forehead. He shifted, paced a few steps, trying to shake the unwelcome thought away.

It was irrelevant. He preferred to deal with reality, with the present. And the pregnancy, deliberate or accidental, was a fact that had to be faced squarely. Besides, she wouldn't have gone to such lengths…would she?

Liz ignored the faint tremor in her fingers as she studied Bob Smyth's chart. His temperature had stabilised during the day. The new antibiotics were obviously doing the job, clearing his lungs, easing his breathing. Microbiology results on the sputum still weren't back, but there was no sign now of the respiratory distress he'd been admitted with the day before yesterday.

She looked at the patient propped up on the pillows, his face relaxed in sleep, and toyed briefly with the thought of disturbing him. Hard plastic dug into her flesh as she pressed her palms on either side of the chart board. Why couldn't Bob have been awake? She could have asked him a question, chatted for a few minutes about something, anything. Then she might have felt as though she was here for some purpose.

Instead, she had to admit to herself that she was avoiding the moment when she had to face Jack. Her husband…the father of her baby. Her heart squeezed painfully as she smoothed a hand over her stomach.

The *unwilling* father of her baby.

She hooked the chart on the end of the bed, her fingers fiddling with the clip for a moment longer. She was hiding, trying to delay the inevitable. Stupid because there was nothing she'd like more than to be able to go home and put her feet up, or perhaps wallow in a bath. If it weren't for Jack being at the house, she'd probably have left the hospital hours ago.

With a small sigh of defeat, she turned to leave the room. Back at the front desk, she wrote up a request for physiotherapy for Bob and slipped it into a wire basket at the end of the desk.

She felt Jack's gaze follow her as she went through to hang up her white coat and retrieve her bag from the locker.

'I need to go to the supermarket on the way home,' she said when she returned.

Jack fell into step with her. 'What for?'

His hand came to rest in the curve of her back as he guided her down the corridor. The small, almost protective gesture sent her pulse into overdrive, scattering her thoughts. 'I'm sorry?'

'What do you need to go to the supermarket for?'

'Oh. Um, yes.' With an effort she pulled her mind back to the conversation. 'You didn't let me know you were coming home so I haven't done any shopping.'

'Hmm.'

The noncommittal response, coupled with her reaction to his touch, irritated her. 'I'm assuming you do want to eat?'

'Yeah, I do. I've got it under control.'

A short time later and they were on the road. *Going home... together.* Liz's heart thumped with an upsurge of poignant emotion.

'Congratulations, by the way.' She clasped her palms together in her lap, interlaced fingers pressing hard into her knuckles. With her peripheral vision, she saw Jack give her a quick glance before returning his eyes to the road.

'For?' He sounded wary.

'Being appointed brigade captain.' She caught her breath in the short, tense silence. 'Why? Is there something else you haven't you bothered to tell me?'

'Liz—'

'Of course, I'd heard rumours. But nobody thought to *tell* me because they naturally assumed I already knew.' She stared at his profile, hating the bitterness she could hear in her voice. 'How do you think that made me feel, Jack?'

He sighed. 'I thought I'd be home to tell you before the details got out. I should have known better. I'm sorry.'

A muscle jumped along the line of his now clean-shaven jaw. He looked disgustingly fresh and well rested.

And utterly desirable.

While she felt frumpy and unattractive. She wrenched her gaze away, sealing her lips to stop herself from saying anything more.

As soon as the car stopped in the driveway, she scrambled out and opened the back door of the car.

'Leave those,' Jack said from the driver's side as she reached for one of the grocery bags on the back seat.

'I'm here so I might as well carry something.' She leaned in and grasped a calico handle.

Moments later, hands clamped around her hips and she was gently but firmly tugged out of the vehicle. The bag she held was removed. Off balance from his touch, she looked up to find hard blue eyes boring into hers. 'I said leave them. Just…go inside and put your feet up. Do whatever you like, but let someone else be in charge for a while.'

'Fine, carry them all yourself, then.' With Jack's arms spread, one hand on the car door, the other on the roof, his solidly muscled body effectively corralled her. Her heart ricocheted around in her chest cavity. He'd touched her through layers of clothing, but the imprint of his strong hands still lingered on her flesh. Even worse was her body's wicked yearning to press against him. She curled her fingers around her handbag to stop any possibility of reaching out.

Her eyes fixed on the navy rib of his neckband, she forced her mind to form a coherent sentence. 'If you'll get out of my way, I'll leave you to it.'

Letting go of the car door, he shifted enough for her to brush past.

Not trusting her voice while he was still so close, she shot a tight smile in his direction. Then, mustering all the dignity she could, she walked towards the house.

'I put the key back in the pot-belly if you need it.' His voice followed her up the path.

A few moments later he joined her on the veranda, shopping bags in hand. 'Dinner will be in an hour or so. I'll call you.'

'Fine,' she mumbled, fumbling through the contents of her bag for her keys. She should have just retrieved the spare from the wretched stove. That way she'd have been inside already and out of his disturbing radius.

He shifted his weight, hefting the bags. Out of the corner of her eye she could see his biceps bulging slightly, filling the short sleeve of his T-shirt. 'Do you want me to get the spare?'

She started at the sound of his voice as her fingers closed around her keyring.

'No.' Picking one, she stabbed it into the lock, relieved when it turned smoothly.

'After you.' She pushed the door open and stood back to hold the screen. The tang of his aftershave stayed with her as she stood on the doorstep, staring after him.

The thin cotton knit shirt moulded to his long back. She'd always loved his broad shoulders, loved the strength in them. With snug jeans clinging to narrow hips, he was heart-throb material. A hot spear of lust twisted in her abdomen. Her shoulders slumped and she closed her eyes on a wave of despair. Even after their years together, even after the bitter arguments that had punctuated their relationship before he'd gone away, she wasn't immune to his masculine appeal. In fact, she wondered if she'd become even more sensitised to him in his absence. For the sake of her sanity she hoped familiarity would breed its contempt—and quickly.

'Are you all right?' Jack's voice jolted her out of her miserable reverie. 'Do you need a hand?'

'Yes. No.' She drew herself up. The last thing she needed

right now was for him to touch her again. 'I'm fine, thank you. It's… I'll go and, um, have a bath. Now. In the en suite.'

She fled, feeling his gaze follow her into the house, only releasing her when she turned into the main bedroom.

An hour later, more pampered than she'd felt in a long time, she wandered through to the kitchen.

'Good timing.' He looked up from the bench where he was putting the finishing touches on a colourful tossed salad. She fidgeted beneath his scrutiny. 'You look better. Less exhausted.'

She grimaced wryly. 'Thanks, I guess.'

'You always look beautiful, Liz.' A small smile curled the edges of his lips. She dragged her eyes away to focus on the chunks of tomato dotted over the lettuce.

'I wasn't fishing for a compliment.' But in her heart she wondered if she was telling the entire truth. Some small, stubborn core lapped up the words, wanting more. *Really dumb.* They'd soon be going their separate ways… They had to. The marriage was over. She couldn't use the pregnancy to hold him. Wanting more of anything from him was pointless.

He shrugged. 'I've set the table on the deck and poured you a drink.' He nodded at a wineglass filled with golden liquid. 'Why don't you take that outside and sit down while I put the salmon on?'

'I can't drink alcohol.'

'I know.' He opened the sliding door with his elbow while balancing the salad in one hand and plates in the other. 'It's apple cider. Non-alcoholic.'

'Oh. Then…thanks.' She picked up the chilled glass and stood awkwardly.

'Coming out?' He was waiting at the door.

'Can I do anything?'

'Yep. Grab the salad.' He held out the bowl. As soon as she'd taken it, he turned away to the barbecue. 'Sit. Relax.'

The smell of salmon sizzling on the hot barbecue plate made Liz acutely aware of how hungry she was. She rearranged the table to make room for the things she carried then slid onto the seat. A jaw-cracking yawn caught her by surprise. She hastily smothered the last of it when she realised Jack was watching.

'Excuse me.'

'Early night for you tonight.'

'Yes.' She sighed, lounging back on her chair and stretching out her legs. 'I must. I'm on call.'

'No. You're not.'

His response didn't make sense. She frowned. 'I'm rostered on.'

'Tony changed it.'

'Tony changed it?' Perplexed, she sat for a long moment until the implications sank in. She bolted upright, her hands fisted. 'Tony changed it! After you talked to him?'

'Mmm. But all I—'

'I can't believe you would do that. What made you think you have the right? If you think you can come back here after all that time away and pull this heavy-handed husband rubbish then you can think again. I won't tolerate it. You…you…' She threw her hands up. 'Words fail me.'

'Not noticeably, darlin',' he drawled, his expression shuttered as he walked past her back into the house.

She marched after him. 'You've never been the nannying sort, Jack, and I don't appreciate you starting now.'

Heat wafted over her as Jack opened the oven and used mitts to retrieve two baked potatoes.

'Don't you?' A muscle flexed in his jaw. 'If you're not going to be more sensible with your health, you'll have to get used to it.'

She gaped at his profile for long seconds. 'That's a stupid thing to say. I *am* sensible with my health. I'm a doctor, for goodness' sake.'

'The two things don't necessarily go hand in hand, sweet-heart.' He swiped off the mitts and dropped them on the bench. With his hands on his hips, he slanted a dark, brooding look at her. 'I've been back in the country for half a day and I know that you've worked hours that would stop a normal person in their tracks. And the contents of our fridge would only have kept a dieting rabbit happy for a couple of hours.'

He picked up the plate with the potatoes and she was left with a view of his back as he walked away from her again. Even with frustration stampeding through her, she couldn't help an involuntary scan down his lean length. Abruptly, the anger turned to a visceral tug of desire. How she used to delight in running her hands over his body, the swimmer's shoulders, the narrow waist, hard, muscular buttocks.

She took a deep breath, desperately channelling her energy to a more appropriate avenue. They were arguing about food. She followed him out to the barbecue where he turned the salmon.

'Like I said before, if you'd seen fit to let me know you were coming, I might have had a chance to lay in supplies for a whole bloody warren.' She sounded inadequate and defensive while he looked so big and gorgeous and in control. It wasn't fair. He was the interloper here.

The corners of his mouth twitched. If he laughed at her she was going to dump the salad over his head.

'I know. The point is there wasn't enough in our fridge to feed one overworked doctor. Which confirms that you've been working long hours as you haven't had time to restock.' He flipped the browned fillets onto the serving plate. 'Dinner's ready.'

'It's not that. I've been tired.' Aware she sounded more like a petulant child than an adult, she slipped into her seat. She knew if she'd been home alone there was a good chance she'd have opened a tin of baked beans and then gone to bed.

'I rest my case.' He picked up the bottle of red wine and topped up his glass before giving her an old-fashioned look over the rim.

She fumed silently for a long moment. 'Anyway, that's beside the point. You have no right to interfere in my professional life. I've a good mind to ring Tony and insist he reinstate the roster.'

Jack sighed. 'I didn't *ask* him to change it, Liz. It was his call. His *professional* decision. And one I happen to agree with.'

'Why would he do it without telling me?'

'I was there when he made the decision and I said I'd let you know. We were talking about last night's accident, as new fire chief to hospital superintendent. It prompted him to remember you'd been on duty. There are four other doctors at the hospital.'

'Two. Barbara's on holiday and Tim's just broken his leg,' she muttered.

'Nevertheless, someone else is doing tonight's shift.' He pushed the salad bowl towards her before reaching across to add a piece of fish and baked potato to her plate. 'Now, can we eat?'

The meal looked perfect. *Perfect.* She'd had the workday from hell. All her personal relationships were a disaster. Her brother, Mark, was angry because she'd tried to talk him out of his latest hare-brained stunt. Her mother was disappointed in her because she hadn't succeeded with her brother. She was pregnant, married to a man who didn't want to be a father. And now the man wanted to play happy families as though nothing out of the ordinary was happening.

The perfection in front of her seemed to underline the wretched state of everything else.

She stared at tiny brown granules of pepper showering over the food on Jack's plate as he twisted the top of the grinder.

His eyes met hers as he slowly placed the unit back on the table. 'Is there a problem? I never thought to ask you if there's anything you can't eat.'

'The salmon's fine. It's not that…it's you.' She swallowed, trying to subdue the undulation in her stomach. 'It's this whole weird thing. We agreed to a divorce. Why are you behaving as though you're trying out for husband of the year when we both know our marriage is in the ditch?'

'I know what we agreed on. But we're not divorced yet and maybe we don't have to be.' He leaned forward and rested his elbows on the table, his eyes guarded as they held hers. 'But if we're going to fix our marriage, someone has to start somewhere.'

'And you think you're that someone?' A year, even six months ago, his stand would have been the sweetest offer he could have made. But the fact remained he'd been adamant about their marriage remaining child-free back then. All that had changed was her pregnancy. If he stayed now, it smacked of self-sacrifice. She didn't want that for her baby. Or herself. 'What if *I* don't believe it can be fixed? What if…I don't want you back?' she finished in a rush so the words wouldn't choke her.

If she hadn't been looking at him, she'd have missed any sign her words had registered. As it was, there was just the suggestion of stillness in his face, a tightening around the eyes, his throat moving in a quick swallow. She had an urge to push harder, see what it took to make him feel the turmoil she was feeling.

'But you're not sure.' He picked up his napkin and laid it on his lap.

'W-why do you say that?'

He gave her a bland look. 'You haven't told anyone we're separated.'

'How do you know?'

'Among other things, I ran into your mother at the supermarket this afternoon. If she knew my days were numbered

I don't think she'd have been able to resist some small barb to let me know.'

She stared at him, unable to refute the claim. Her mother's antipathy towards Jack had caused difficulty from the beginning of their marriage. Any sign that the union was over and her mother wouldn't hesitate to voice her pleasure.

'So why haven't you?' Jack interrupted her thoughts.

'Because… Because…' She searched for a reason that would set him back on his heels. Instead, her shoulders slumped as the anger seeped out of her. 'Because an opportunity never seemed to present itself. And then I found out I was pregnant and it seemed even less appropriate.'

She reached for the base of her glass, the liquid sloshing slightly as she pushed it to and fro.

'It's hardly the sort of thing I could share without making some sort of explanation, is it? What was I supposed to say? *Hey, everyone! Guess what? Jack and I have decided to get a divorce. Oh, and by the way, in case you hadn't noticed, I'm pregnant. Isn't it just peachy?*' She grimaced. 'Hell, Jack, I'm a doctor. If *I* can't get birth control right, what sort of example am I to my patients?'

'Must have been tough for you.' Jack gave her an understanding smile, which slowly faded when she frowned at him.

He reached for her hand, stopping the restless movement of the glass. His thumb caressed her wedding ring, rubbing her skin lightly on either side. The warmth of his touch felt good, made her realise how chilled her fingers were.

'Liz, let's leave this for another time.'

'I won't change my mind.' Her voice sounded wobbly, hoarse. She had to be strong. Hers wasn't the only life affected by her decisions any more.

'I know.'

She sucked her lips between her teeth to quell their trembling. 'Then what's the point?'

'The point is you're tired, I'm still jet-lagged.' He smiled in appeal. 'I promise we can resume hostilities after a good night's sleep. Scalpels at dawn. Cross my heart.'

A snorting half-laugh escaped before she could stop it. 'I hate that you can make me see the absurdity of this when I'm still mad as hell with you.'

'I know.' He grinned.

'There're a lot of things that need to be said.' Still reluctant to be charmed by him, she said, 'Serious things that you can't smooth over with a bit of a joke, Jack.'

'Yes, but there's no rule that says we have to say all those things tonight, is there?' He stroked her knuckles, his blue eyes held an engaging appeal. 'Truce?'

She contemplated him in silence, common sense and exhaustion waging a short war with her need to settle her future—their future—one way or the other. 'All right. Until tomorrow.'

'I'll consider myself on notice.' He gave her hand a quick squeeze before releasing it and lifting his glass to chink it lightly on the edge of hers. 'Until tomorrow.'

The uneasy peace held until the end of the meal. Jack seemed to put himself out to enchant her in a way that he hadn't since the very early days of their whirlwind courtship and spur-of-the-moment marriage.

She pushed her plate away and sat back. The spring evening was chilling slightly, but she felt too lethargic to bother getting a cardigan. Moving might somehow break the spell that kept them in this civilised cocoon. And she was enjoying this reminder of her romance with Jack, a brief interlude before reality intruded again. She smiled slightly as the baby kicked against the hand she'd just rested in her lap. Not all reality was content to be ignored.

'I spoke to Danny McIntyre,' said Jack, breaking the companionable silence.

'Did you?' The lovely warm glow from her thoughts winked

out abruptly. She met his eyes as she rubbed her stomach gently, trying to soothe the little being within.

'The accident this morning sounded bad.'

'Yes. I thought you didn't want to argue,' she said in a vain effort to stop the discussion. Might as well ask her unborn babe to stop using her bladder for football practice.

'I don't. We're not.'

She wasn't fooled by his conversational tone. 'So you get to choose a topic but I don't? Maybe *I* don't want to discuss *this* topic.'

'Is that because you broke the first rule of first aid at the accident scene?'

'Did Danny say that?'

'No.' He smiled slightly. 'What Danny did was give me a glowing description of your courage as the car teetered on the bridge.'

'Hardly teetering. By the time I got there they had the car stabilised. They were just waiting for the jaws-of-life.' She frowned. 'You didn't give Danny a hard time about this, did you?'

He ignored her question. 'But it was still on the edge of the bridge. You shouldn't have put yourself at risk.'

'I made a judgement call. The woman was making her injuries worse by moving around,' said Liz, her heart pounding. She'd been so afraid for the young victim. No force on earth could have prevented her from getting into that car. 'What was I supposed to do? Leave her alone there until she severed something vital on a jagged edge? She was pregnant and afraid she was losing her baby, Jack.'

'Is that why you did it?' he asked softly after a moment. His eyes were dark, hard to read. 'Because she was pregnant? Because you were viewing the situation as a fellow mother-to-be rather than a doctor?'

'Yes. Is that so bad?' But she already knew the rational answer. A responder putting themselves at risk at an accident could very well end up becoming another victim, making more work for others at the scene.

'It could have been if something had gone wrong.'

'Nothing did.' His criticism of her actions hurt more than she'd thought possible. That he was right didn't help. 'You always say there's no point dealing in could-have-beens.'

'I also believe in reviewing ops afterwards and seeing where we could have been more effective.'

'I was effective and I didn't get hurt.' Unable to sit any longer, she stood, picking up her plate and reaching for his, only to find both of them whisked out of her hands.

'I'll look after the dishes.'

'I'm capable of carrying a few plates.' She loitered beside her chair, heaviness dragging at her limbs.

'Sure, but you don't need to tonight. Go and sit down.' He stacked the plates and scooped up the empty glasses before glancing up to find her standing in the same spot. 'Are you still here?'

'I—I think I'll go to bed.'

'Good idea. Take the master bedroom. I've put fresh sheets on the bed.'

Quick heat burned her cheeks as she remembered their exchange of words earlier. 'Thanks.'

'Hell, Liz. I didn't mean that the way it must have sounded.'

'It doesn't matter.' She waved a hand in dismissal and forced her leaden legs to move. 'Goodnight.'

It did matter.

Jack blew out a breath of frustration and guilt after she'd gone. He'd seen her face fall, a tell-tale blush briefly hiding the pallor of fatigue. The quip about the sheets had been un-intentional. Sure, he'd had some harsh thoughts while he'd been making the bed up. But common sense told him, as much as he burned to sleep with his wife, it wasn't going to happen while they had so much unresolved. Though he'd have been happy to put forward an argument on how it might help them resolve their problems… But then, that was how Liz had ended up pregnant in the first place, so perhaps not. Sharing a bed with Liz was probably a long way down the track.

He dropped the dishes in the sink and looked out at the gathering twilight. His sanity might be in question before this was over. The thought of her in bed on the other side of the house made him ache.

He'd come home to save his marriage, prepared to *talk* about having a family if that's what it took. There should have been discussions, reconciliations—he'd especially been looking forward to those. But they were supposed to ease into it, approach the problem like mature adults, set a timetable that they could both be happy with. There should have been a decision to stop using contraception, the fun of trying to conceive and, eventually—maybe—Liz falling pregnant. Not this headlong pitch into impending parenthood.

He wasn't ready.

Which made him realise that the problem with his imaginary future was that he'd never truly envisaged a pregnant Liz, the birth of a child.

Himself as a father.

And yet once his younger self had wanted that role fervently until grief and betrayal had crushed the naive joy in his heart.

Suds filled the sink as he squirted detergent under the running tap. Could he resurrect an echo of that anticipation for Liz, for the child they were going to have together? If anyone deserved his best efforts, it was his wife. But contemplating their future as parents left him cold and empty.

He sighed and began methodically washing the plates. After his experiences with his manipulative mother and then with his unfaithful fiancée's pregnancy, he'd vowed to squash every nurturing instinct he possessed. For the first time he understood how thoroughly successful he'd been. Poor Liz. She'd never agree to take him back if she realised what an appalling candidate for fatherhood he really was. He'd have to work hard to make sure she never found out.

CHAPTER THREE

IN THE bedroom, Liz shut the door and closed her eyes as she leaned her forehead against the wood. The faint clinking of china carried to her. Jack working in the kitchen.

Jack.

Rolling her head, she twisted until her back was pressed to the door. She opened her eyes. The first thing she saw was the bed.

One area they'd never had trouble in…until now.

Blinking hard, she sniffed back the tears that pressed for release. Not that she wanted to sleep with Jack.

She grimaced. Who was she kidding? She wanted him like crazy with her heart, mind and body.

But everything was too messy. Sleeping with him wouldn't solve anything.

She walked over to turn down the spread and touch the crisp linen pillowcase on her side. Jack making up the bed showed unexpected sensitivity. She should just appreciate it, not feel this tearing pressure in her heart.

He said that he wanted to save their marriage. Something completely out of character. Especially as she was pregnant. She had expected him to run a mile as soon as he saw her condition.

So why wasn't he running? A quick pummelling from inside her abdomen reminded her of the shock on his face in the hospital room. A small, watery chuckle escaped before she quickly sobered. Judging by his reaction, he certainly hadn't had a change of heart about having children.

And after their increasingly acrimonious arguments on the matter before he'd gone away, she'd changed her mind about starting a family with him. Discovering her pregnancy soon after his departure had come as a shock to her too. All that hard thinking she'd done about what sort of man she wanted to be the father of her children was suddenly irrelevant. The bottom line was, Jack was the father and he fell far short of what she wanted for her baby.

A fine situation she'd got herself and her poor unborn child into. Could Jack change? No, it wasn't that simple. His attitude was too entrenched. She had to stop torturing herself with such imaginings. Apart from those few fraught moments in the hospital room right after he'd discovered her pregnancy, he hadn't mentioned their impending parenthood. Just their marriage.

Nothing had changed. Her baby's future was her responsibility and hers alone. A child needed a warm and secure environment. No father at all would surely be better than one who was completely uninterested.

Liz would never subject her baby to a cold, formal childhood like she'd endured.

Now, with her medical training, she understood the psychology behind her drive for perfection and her brother's addiction to extreme sports. In her secret heart, she'd hoped her father might find some value in her. Mark, her brother, must have felt lacking as well, using his dangerous behaviour as a method of seeking their distant parents' attention.

Why hadn't their father loved or valued them? Perhaps he hadn't wanted children at all.

She'd known since high school that her mother must have been pregnant before the marriage. But in her teenage naivety she'd fantasised it had happened because they'd been in love and engaged. Now she wondered if her parents had talked about having a family. Or had they rushed headlong into matrimony without considering the weighty issues? Perhaps she had more in common with her mother than she'd ever have believed possible. Unfortunately, asking was out of the question. Her mother never, ever discussed personal or emotionally untidy things.

Liz frowned. Marrying, almost eloping with Jack, had been fabulously romantic at the time. They'd seemed so attuned to each other, especially in bed. She'd been smug about finding a partner prepared to give her the space to practise her career. In hindsight, she could see they hadn't known nearly enough about each other. Hadn't truly discussed the issue of having children. She realised Jack had made vague comments, let her do the talking whenever she'd brought up the subject. Fool that she was, she'd read the meaning she wanted into his responses.

What were Jack's reasons for not wanting children? In all their arguments he'd skirted the issue every time. If he was serious about saving their marriage, fatherhood was part of the deal.

She stripped off the oversized T-shirt and track pants and studied her reflection in the mirror for a long moment. She looked pregnant, but nowhere near as enormous as she felt. When she was in her white coat at work, the nurses assured her that her pregnancy was barely noticeable. And yet in the last couple of weeks she felt like she'd ballooned. She ran her hand over the mound. Fourteen more weeks. The skin felt ready to split now. How much more could it stretch? She reached for the moisturiser and massaged more cream into the tight skin, smiling when the pummelling seemed to follow the movement of her hand. A baby. She was growing a baby, a little girl. Almost certainly a little brunette since she and Jack both had dark hair. But would she have Jack's blue eyes or her hazel ones? Not that it was important. What mattered was this little girl had a mother who loved her to distraction, sight unseen.

His muscles pleasantly tired after a long run, Jack scooped up the morning newspaper off the veranda and let himself into the house quietly in case Liz was still asleep. He needn't have worried. The door of the main bedroom was open and the bed already neatly made up. No sign of Liz. He found her at the kitchen bench, eating a bowl of cereal. When she turned towards him, sunlight from the side window gilded her profile.

'God, it's true.' Fresh shock rippled through him as he took in her swollen abdomen. The thin fabric of her red top was stretched so tightly across the bulge that he could see her belly button protruding like some sort of tiny stem. 'You really *are* pregnant.'

'Brilliant observation.'

His gaze shifted upwards when the quick breath she sighed out moved her breasts gently. He realised for the first time how much larger they were. Pregnancy had made his wife, who'd always been on the small side, positively voluptuous. Were they tender? He wanted to touch, to caress. To sink his lips onto the soft, creamy flesh. His heart skipped a beat then set an uncomfortable rhythm of hard, fast thuds.

'Didn't it sink in yesterday, Jack? Maybe you hoped you'd dreamed it.'

'Dreamed what?' He blinked, trying to clear the direction of his thoughts as he dragged his gaze from her cleavage back to her face.

Liz gave him a strange look. 'The pregnancy.'

'Oh, that. No. No, I just...' He could feel heat gathering across his cheekbones. 'It did sink in. It just didn't really...sink in.' God, he sounded so lame. 'It takes some getting used to.'

'I suppose so,' she said, her voice flat as she turned away from him. She rinsed her plate and left it on the sink to be washed.

'Do you want me to cook you some breakfast?'

'No. Thanks. I—I want to get to the hospital early.' Drying her hands, she moved away from the sink.

Jack kept his eyes fixed firmly on her face, relieved when his pulse began to level off with his mind on less provocative subjects. 'It's only half past seven. Aren't you supposed to be eating for two?'

'Only if you want me to be the size of a barn instead of a small house.'

'Are you larger than you should be?' His pulse jumped again this time on a surge of fear. According to his mother, he'd been a very large baby and giving birth to him had nearly killed her. Could having his baby put Liz at risk? She was such a dynamo he tended to forget she was tiny. He frowned. 'Isn't that dangerous? Have you been to the doctor? What did he say?'

'Yes, I have been to the doctor. No, it isn't dangerous. And I'm the right size, thank you for asking.' She was very nearly pouting.

'I've upset you.' He wanted to take her in his arms, comfort her, promise her he'd fix everything. But as he was part of the problem here, she wouldn't be impressed by words. He needed to prove he'd go the distance with her. Time was his best ally.

'Not really.' She huffed out a breath. 'It's one thing for me to feel enormous, it's another thing for you to tell me that I look it. Especially since…'

'Especially since I got you in that condition in the first place?' he finished for her. But at the time he'd been looking for the simple pleasure that came with their tentative reconciliation. Nothing more. 'I didn't do it deliberately, Liz, and I seem to remember the occasion as mutually pleasurable.'

'Well, I certainly didn't. Get pregnant deliberately, I mean.' She moved closer and poked him in the sternum to emphasise her point. 'That's what you think, isn't it? That *I* messed up the precautions.'

With her so close, keeping his eyes away from her cleavage took a conscious effort. 'Not deliberately, perhaps.'

'Oh, you think I did it subconsciously? That's so much better. How magnanimous of you.' Her eyes narrowed as she tilted her head to glare up at him. 'I would never bring a child into a household where one parent doesn't want it. But if I *had* decided to go behind your back on this, don't you think I'd have *accidentally* fallen pregnant while there was still a chance for our marriage? How dumb to wait until we're teetering on the verge of divorce and you're about to fly off to the other side of the world.'

'Did you know before I went away?'

'No, I didn't.' Her breasts rose and fell with her sigh. 'Though I can see that there were some signs, but I put them down to other things.'

'But you must have known soon after I left. When were you going to tell me about…it?'

'About…*it*?' she said, arching a brow at him. 'You mean about the baby?'

'Yes.' Tightness gathered in his chest as he waited for her answer.

Finally, she gave him a helpless look and slowly shook her head. 'I don't know. I think I hoped you'd just…stay away, go on fighting other people's fires indefinitely. It was stupid.'

'Didn't you think I had a right to know?' He should stop pushing. Sooner or later, she would say something he didn't want to hear. But he could help himself.

'Did you?' She crossed her arms defensively. The action pushed the disturbing cleavage into even more prominence. 'You'd made your position abundantly clear before you left. There didn't seem to be any room for negotiation.'

'But this…' he waved a hand towards her stomach '…changes things.'

'It does for me, yes.' She tilted her chin at him defiantly. 'I wanted a baby and now I'm having one.'

The band around his heart squeezed harder. 'It changes things for me, too, Liz.'

She pounced as soon as the words were out of his mouth. 'Are you saying you want this baby?'

His brain refused to co-operate. He opened his mouth, hoping the right words would be uttered magically. 'I…I'm—'

'Don't bother straining yourself for a reply to placate me.' She held up her hand, disgust patent on her face. 'I can see the answer for myself.'

'No, dammit, you can't.' He reached out to stop her as she stalked past him. With his hand circling her upper arm loosely, the backs of his fingers were nestled against the soft, warm flesh of her right breast.

She gasped, raising startled hazel eyes to his. Her pupils flared dark and deep, betraying her involuntary reaction, giving him the unexpected knowledge that she wasn't as contained as she was trying to appear. Hope and exultation surged through him, a palpable force loosening the pain in his chest.

'Give me a chance,' he said, softening his voice persuasively. 'I need time to get used to the idea. You've known for months. I've known for a bare twenty-four hours.'

'And what if you can't *get used* to the idea, Jack?' She wrested her arm out of his grip, rubbing the skin as though trying to scrub away the evidence of his touch. 'This is a baby. Not a ten-day trial where you get a refund if you change your mind.'

'I know that.' He ground his teeth. God, he probably knew it almost better than she did. 'I'm prepared to do the right thing.'

'That's big of you, isn't it? Forgive me if I don't fall down on my knees to offer up prayers of gratitude.' She looked at him stonily. 'I don't want my child to have a duty father.'

'And I don't want it to have an endless parade of *uncles* through its life when it has a perfectly good father around.' The irony of his words blasted into the silence and he couldn't suppress a wry grin. 'Well, perhaps an imperfectly good father.'

Liz stared at him for a long moment. Then her lips twitched, only to immediately thin. She was obviously not prepared to let a smile escape. 'It depends on the imperfection, doesn't it?'

He felt his smile slip as the cold vice around his heart clenched again. 'Yeah, I guess it does.'

'Look, this isn't getting us anywhere, and I really do have to go to work now. Can we pick it up later?'

'Sure.' He watched her walk out the door before rubbing a hand over his face in defeat. She was right. He wasn't good enough. Even without knowing his history, she could sense that lack in him.

'Grace Burns?' Liz scanned the room for her first patient, a four-year-old according to the notes.

A mountain of a man stood up, his muscular, tattooed arms cradling a small blonde urchin.

'Come through, Mr Burns.' She led the way into the cubicle and shut the door. 'I'm Liz Campbell. Have a seat.'

Liz slid onto a second chair and smiled at the child. 'Hello, Grace. Tell me why you've come to see me today.'

'I got somefing in my ear.' Solemn blue eyes were wide with caution.

'Have you? How did it get there?'

'I put it dere.' Golden ringlets bobbed as she tilted her head to look up at her father. 'Didn't I, Daddy?'

Liz suppressed a smile. Grace was adorable.

'I found her in my wife's studio with the bead box, Doc.

She must have got in while I was getting the other kids off to school.' The man spoke quickly, obviously nervous. 'I managed to get one of the beads out, but I couldn't reach the red one. And Gracie said it was hurting.'

'Let's have a look, then, shall we, Grace?'

The girl watched with saucer-like eyes as Liz picked up the otoscope and attached a speculum. 'I'm going to shine this light and look inside your ear through this magnifying glass. See?'

Grace squinted at the instrument doubtfully.

'I need you to keep very still for me. Can you do that, Grace?'

'Will it hurt?'

'It shouldn't, but I want you to tell me if it does, okay?'

Grace checked with her father for reassurance. His smile must have given it because the big blue eyes swivelled back to Liz and the blonde head nodded.

Using a pair of forceps, Liz extracted the red bead easily and dropped it into a waiting kidney dish.

'Hmm, you've got something else in here, Grace,' she said, examining the ear canal again before carefully probing with the forceps.

'Ow. It hurts now.'

'Okay.' Liz straightened up, addressing the girl's father. 'It's very deep and the skin around it is quite red so whatever it is has probably been there a while. I think we'll use light sedation to make it easier for Grace. Are you happy to hold the anaesthetic mask? I can call the nurse in if you'd prefer.'

After a tiny hesitation, he said, 'No, I can do it.'

'Sure?'

'Yes.'

Liz smiled reassuringly then looked back at the urchin. 'We're going to put this mask on you, Grace. You'll feel sleepy for a few minutes and when you wake up again your ear will feel much better.'

A hand that looked as though it'd be more at home with a

spanner or a plough held the mask over Grace's nose and mouth. The man's gravelly voice murmured words of reassurance and his free hand stroked the girl's hair gently as she lay on the bed.

'That's got it,' said Liz moments later as she pulled the suction tube out of the ear. A small grey lump dropped into the dish as the vacuum was switched off. 'You can take the mask away now.'

'What is it?'

'It looks like a seed of some sort. Maybe from an apple. I'll check her other ear and nostrils just in case she's been busy there too.'

When she'd finished, Liz stripped off her gloves and reached for a prescription pad. 'I'll give you a script for antibiotic drops to put in her ear three times a day for a week to settle down that inflammation. And I'd like you to bring her back early next week so we can check to make sure it's resolved.'

'Okay.'

Liz smiled at the waking child. 'And I want you to leave the beads for Mummy, okay, Grace?'

Another solemn nod, this one a little sleepy.

'She will. We'll be putting a higher bolt on the door as soon as we get home, won't we, Gracie?' The unlikely-looking father scooped the girl up and she immediately buried her face in the crook of his shoulder. 'Thanks, Doc.'

Liz sat for a few moments after the pair had gone, thinking about this morning's scene with Jack, remembering his wry smile as he'd joked about the sort of father he'd make. For a moment, a bare split second, after she'd rejected his banter, he'd looked so...raw, so vulnerable.

Her fingers massaged circles at her temples, trying to dissipate the headache she could feel forming.

Was she wrong to dictate the sort of parent she wanted him to be?

Was an imperfect father better than none at all?

Better than a *parade of uncles* was what Jack had said. Was that what he'd had in his childhood? It looked like neither of them had had a good father figure. She frowned, trying to remember what she knew about his family. He hadn't talked much about it, but she knew he'd lived with his grandmother for most of his life. At least, that was the impression he'd given her. She realised just how little he'd really told her. They needed to talk, about lots of things, not just the baby.

She huffed out a sharp breath. Nothing was turning out the way she expected. Jack had been back a day and suddenly she was questioning everything she'd resolved in her mind while he'd been away. And the enormity of her neediness was alarming. She had to pull herself together, be strong, be prepared in case their marriage couldn't be saved.

He'd asked her to give him a chance. Did she dare? Her heart would break all over again if he failed and decided fatherhood wasn't for him.

But how could she not take the risk? Didn't her baby deserve a father?

CHAPTER FOUR

THE place looked deserted when Liz arrived home, but evidence of Jack's presence was everywhere outside. In the freshly cut lawn, a pile of tree trimmings and garden rubbish ready to burn. Things she hadn't been able to keep up with because of work and tiredness from the pregnancy.

And inside the house the delicious smell of tomatoes, herbs and garlic wafted from the kitchen. She dropped her handbag on the sideboard and crossed to the stove to lift the lid off the cast-iron pot. Rich Bolognese sauce simmered gently.

She'd forgotten how wonderful it was to come home to prepared meals. At the beginning of their marriage Jack had done the lion's share of the cooking. And he was better at it than she was.

The poignant memory of those honeymoon months brought a tearing lump to her throat. He'd been so caring and considerate. More than that. Nurturing, in a subtle, masculine way. It was one of the things she'd loved about him. Probably one of the reasons she'd gone along with the crazy idea to marry on the spur of the moment while they were on holiday.

She'd travelled to New Zealand as Dr Elizabeth Dustin and flown home as Mrs Jack Campbell. The trouble had started when she'd become broody just over a year later. On some deep, deep biological level, she must have pegged him as great father material, which made his adamant refusal to consider having children such a shock. Had she missed clues to the way he felt? She didn't think so, but in hindsight she could see how precious little he'd told her in the honeymoon phase of their relationship. He was good at hiding himself in plain view.

Even when they'd started arguing about starting a family, she'd been convinced that if she could just come up with the right approach, the magical combination of words, he'd capitulate. No wonder he thought she'd got pregnant on purpose.

She sniffed deeply, wiping her cheeks dry. Pregnancy was turning her into a regular leaking faucet. Instead of standing here weeping over a saucepan, she needed to find Jack and ask him about the *uncles*.

She turned to walk away from the stove and immediately faltered to a standstill as she saw the dining table for the first time. Pressure in her chest made it hard to breathe. Two long cream candles waited for a match to touch their elegant tapered tips. And, in the space between them, a cluster of rich red rosebuds.

The setting screamed Jack Campbell bent on romance…seduction. Her knees wobbled. Part of her yearned to surrender. Yearned to be held by him, to ignore the things that stood between them. But she couldn't…wouldn't. Her future and the future of her baby depended on it.

She had a feeling she was on the verge of discovering crucial information about her husband, that there was a real clue in his unguarded words from this morning. If she probed carefully, she might learn why he was so against having children.

On the way through the hall she checked her reflection in the mirror. Eyes not too red, just a little glassy. Cheeks pale. She scrubbed them lightly before walking purposefully down to the back door.

The fire service four-wheel drive was standing outside the shed, which meant Jack was probably working inside. She hesitated, debating whether to leave her questions until he came back to the house. But his comment had been niggling at her on and off all day, and they had to start talking some time. Why not now?

She found him at the bench bent over their portable fire-fighting pump. The threadbare material of faded jeans strained over his buttocks. An oily rag hanging from the patch pocket draped over the masculine curve. Grease and dirt liberally smeared his skin and clothes and a dark V of sweat stained the tattered singlet where it stretched beneath his armpit. Still unshaven, the stubble on his profile gave him a tough, edgy look. Even dressed as he was, he oozed sex appeal and Liz couldn't suppress the tide of warmth that raced through her system in response.

He lifted the hem of his top to wipe his forehead. The side view of his long, lean stomach above the low-slung jeans had her greeting stuttering to a halt.

'Jack.' The constriction in her throat made her voice sound strangled.

His hands lowered the fabric of the singlet over the disturbing torso as he turned to face her.

'Liz.' A slow smile lit his face and her heart lurched. God, she'd forgotten how special he could make her feel with just a look. 'I didn't hear you come home.'

She swallowed, tried to gather her thoughts. 'You weren't in the house.'

'The fire pump's overdue for a service.' He focussed intently on her face. 'Have you been crying?'

'Not...really. It's just hormones.' The choking lump started to swell again in her throat. 'I saw the way you'd set the table.'

He tilted his head, eyes twinkling at her. 'Cutlery wasn't laid out right, huh?'

She chuckled, relieved to feel the need to cry recede. 'Ah,

should I have checked that?' Her smile slipped and she looked at him seriously for a moment. 'The table looks gorgeous... romantic.'

'Thanks.'

'Jack...we need to talk.' She tried hard to make it sound non-threatening, persuasive. But the wary look glazing his eyes told her she hadn't succeeded. Liz's spirits plummeted again with the sudden loss of connection between them.

'About?' He picked up a ratchet and selected a socket. After studying it briefly, he put it back and chose another.

She suppressed a sigh. 'Please tell me about your uncles.'

'Uncle Ron?' Dark blue eyes glanced her way then away again. 'Haven't seen him yet. How is he?' Tool in hand, he slotted his arms into the machine.

'He's doing well. So is Aunty Peg. I saw them last week.' She stepped closer, noticing the sheen of perspiration on his shoulder. 'But I don't mean Uncle Ron, Jack. And you know it.'

There was a short pause before his head swivelled back towards her. 'So they know you're pregnant.'

Heat swept up her throat into her cheeks. 'They've only just found out. And I—I asked them not to tell you.'

'Did you?' A tinny scrape punctuated the sentence. Despite his flat, uninformative tone, she had the feeling he was upset.

Guilt stabbed at her. 'I'm sorry, but it seemed like the most sensible thing to do at the time. It wasn't something I wanted to discuss with you on the telephone.' She studied his grim profile. 'Anyway, stop changing the subject. We were talking about your uncles.'

'My parents were only children.' He was being deliberately obtuse.

'This morning you said you didn't want your child brought up by a parade of uncles. I wondered what you meant.'

The ratchet's clackety-clack as he levered the handle energetically backwards and forwards effectively stopped communication. Though maybe it was Jack's way of saying he wasn't going to answer.

Liz stood her ground, unable to help herself from watching his perfectly toned biceps muscles flex and release with each pull. She didn't need to notice things like that about him, damn it. Her teeth ground together as she waited until the noise stopped. 'Well, Jack?'

'Well, Liz?' he mimicked, pulling an odd-shaped nut out of the machine's innards.

Tension banded around her chest. She was fighting for her marriage and all her husband could do was parody her.

'What are you afraid of? What's so terrible about your past and your family that you can't tell me?' She kept her voice steady, calm, refusing to give in to her pain. 'Don't you trust me?'

'That's a bloody stupid conclusion to come to.' He glared at her as he yanked the oily rag out of his back pocket. 'I'd trust you with my life, you know that.'

'But not with your secrets?' she pressed.

He turned his attention back to the gadget in his hand and rubbed the cloth briskly across the metal. 'I just don't see the point of dredging up the past to try to excuse my behaviour in the present. It's crap.'

Liz wanted to seize the rag and nut and toss them out the door. To grab Jack by his sexy singlet and shake him until he told her who he was, where he'd come from, what he was hiding. 'Don't you think it's shaped the person you've become?'

He jammed the oily rag back into his pocket. 'Getting all Freudian on me, babe?'

Liz realised he hadn't called her that since she'd asked him not to. Perhaps he thought he could distract her by using the annoying endearment now.

'No. *Babe.*' She had the satisfaction of seeing him react, the tiniest flinch, quickly suppressed. 'I'm trying to understand you.'

'What's to understand?' He held the nut up to the light and squinted at it before blowing on it sharply. His face was hard when he looked at her again. 'What you see is what you get.'

'But that's not true, is it? On the surface you seem like a patient, drop-dead gorgeous man with a responsible, demanding job. Someone with integrity, who can be relied on in a tight spot.' She watched as he bent to place the nut back into the machine and used the ratchet in quick jerky motions. Again, she waited for the noise to cease. 'Someone who would make a wonderful father. But you're afraid and I think your past has made you that way. I can't help you if you won't tell me. We need to discuss things if we're going to be parents, Jack.'

He snorted out a breath. 'It seems to me we've had the most important discussion.' His gaze slid down to her belly then back to fasten on her eyes. 'You're pregnant and I'm staying around. Ergo, we're going to be parents.' His mouth twisted derisively.

'Yes, but what sort of parents are we going to be? That's the point here.'

He swung to face her, hands on his hips. Six feet of irritated male wanting her out of his domain. 'Look around you, Liz. Now's not a great time for this discussion.'

'*No* time is a *good* time for you, is it?' Anger pulsed through tired muscles, giving Liz a much-needed energy boost. 'And I'm sick of it, Jack. Do you realise that you've *never* really talked to me?'

He thrust his fingers though his hair, leaving spikes standing in their wake. 'We talk.'

'Never about the important stuff. Never. All I've had from you are edited snippets of your life. Carefully censored titbits so I don't learn too much. So I can't get too close to the real Jack Campbell.'

His face twisted as though he was in pain. Liz could feel her features screwing up in sympathy. 'Not true. Hell, Liz. You *are* close to me. I love you.' His voice was heart-breakingly hoarse. 'You know that.'

She shook her head in sorrow, exhaustion suddenly swamping her. 'Then that's sad, Jack. Because you keep me at such a distance, it doesn't say much for the other relationships in your life.'

He turned aside, braced his hands on the bench. Skin stretched taut and white across his knuckles, contrasting with his tan. She lifted her eyes to his profile. A muscle in his cheek flexed and then stilled.

'Please talk to me. You said you wanted to save our marriage. Bottom line, Jack. Opening up, and I mean *really* opening up, is what it's going to take.' She could hear the desperation, the begging note in her voice. 'Please.'

The silence lengthened.

'Oh, God. You're not going to, are you?' Liz swallowed the bile that rose in her throat. Tears were perilously close and her heart splintered with the agony of them. 'You can't do it. Not even with our marriage on the line.'

His face might have been carved from ash-coloured marble, cold and grey and frozen, for all the effect her words were having on him. She'd never felt so lonely, so empty. As though she'd made a desperate gamble and was learning the full calamity of her loss.

'I'm going inside.' The words rasped out, past the painful tightness in her throat. He didn't move.

Her body quivered with spent emotion, but somehow she managed to turn and walk back towards the house. One foot in front of the other, mind carefully blank. She couldn't break down in front of Jack. Not now.

CHAPTER FIVE

LIZ had gone. Taking her demands with her. Leaving blessed silence in her wake. Jack picked up a screwdriver and waited to feel the relief.

But it didn't come. Instead, he felt...shame.

He'd hurt Liz. Pain had been raw in her voice. She'd begged. *Begged*. And, coward that he was, he still hadn't found the courage to speak.

He threw the tool back on the bench in disgust. Frustration sent him pacing across the concrete towards the house. What the hell was he going to do? He halted, spun around and took the half a dozen steps back to the fire pump. Then stopped again.

He had to find the gumption to talk to Liz. Because of his silence their marriage was combusting, a conflagration that threatened to destroy everything that was good in his life. The only tools he had to save it were words, facts about the past. He took a deep breath.

He had to lay them out for Liz. Ugly as they were. Just give them to her. Trust that she would know what to do with them, *with him*, after they'd been spoken.

He didn't know what he'd do if she found him less worthy once she knew the whole sordid story. The other important women in his life, his mother and his fiancée, hadn't found anything about him worth staying around for.

But he had to take the chance. If he didn't, he was going to lose her anyway.

Before he could change his mind, he strode out of the garage and crossed to the house. His romantic table setting mocked him as he walked through to the hallway.

The door to the main bedroom was closed. He lifted his hand to knock and saw the smears of grease and dirt on his skin. His fingers curling into his palm, he stepped back and huffed out a breath. Now that he'd made the decision, he was almost impatient to get on with the talking—half-afraid his courage would desert him. Still, he couldn't go to Liz like this.

A few minutes later he'd stripped and stepped into the shower. The water jet played directly on the tense muscles of his neck, sluicing down over his shoulders to rinse away the suds as he soaped. If only he could wash away the grime in his past as efficiently as he rinsed the dirt off his body.

He'd always thought of himself as a straightforward sort of a person, someone who had put the past behind, moved on, not dwelled on old pain.

But now he had to face the fact that coping with his mother's vagaries had left its mark, a deeply buried anger about the way she'd treated him and her negligence with her own daughter, his little sister.

Emma.

He squeezed his eyes shut as he remembered the way the two-year old used to toddle towards him, her chubby arms out wide, asking to be picked up. She'd always turned to him rather than Janet if he was around. It hadn't taken her long to learn he was the one most likely to soothe her hurts, clean her up, feed her. That little life had depended on him and he hadn't been there when it had really counted.

She'd been sick when he'd gone to school, but Janet had promised to take her to the doctor. She'd *promised*. By the time he'd got home his little sister had been gravely ill and their mother had been as high as a kite. He'd called an ambulance. The paramedics had given Janet an injection to reverse the effects of the drugs, much to her disgust. Jack had sat in the casualty department of the hospital. Breathing the sickly smell of antiseptic. Listening to his mother's muttered curses behind the cubicle curtain. He'd prayed that the doctors could help his sister. But nothing had pulled little Emma back from the brink of death.

And then there was Kylie. Another memory he hadn't dredged up for years. Teenage lover, mother-to-be, fiancée. She'd been right, or rather her mother had. They'd been way too young to marry and start a family.

Kylie's angry words echoed down the years. She'd thrown her infidelity at him, taunted him with the fact that the baby she'd just miscarried hadn't been his.

But he'd wanted that baby so much, been utterly stricken by its loss. And then he'd had to struggle with grief that didn't go away just because he'd found out that his best friend was the father. One minute he'd nearly been a husband and father and the next…nothing.

For the first time he wondered if he'd been so determined to look after his pregnant fiancée as a way of atoning for not saving Emma.

Once Kylie had dumped him, he'd put it out of his mind, determined to move on.

No looking back.

Ever.

But now that was exactly what Liz wanted him to do. What he had to do to save his marriage.

God knew why people thought it helped to talk about the past. He was only contemplating talking to Liz and he felt sick to his stomach. If thinking about it made him feel this bad, how would actually speaking make him feel?

Facing a large going fire with nothing but his bare hands

seemed an easier option. He turned off the water and reached for the towel.

Dressed and back at Liz's door, Jack rapped lightly on the wood.

No answer. He hesitated a moment, then reached for the handle, pushed the door open. She was curled up on the bed, her back to him. The gentle curves of her body's profile reminded him how he used to love running his hand over her smooth skin, across her ribs, down into the valley at her waist and up onto the bone of her hip.

He walked quietly around the bed, savouring the sight of his sleeping wife for a few precious moments.

The bump of her pregnant belly was only slightly less astounding than it had been that morning. Almost as though she'd been taken over and shaped by something alien. He smiled slightly, thinking that Liz might not appreciate the analogy. In a way, her body had been taken over...by his baby. *His baby.* He moved his tongue in a suddenly dry mouth.

Maybe if he'd been here from the beginning, it wouldn't seem so strange. The changes, the growing, would have been gradual. Pregnancy obviously made her more tired. Napping like this, so easily and particularly when she was upset, was completely out of character.

He frowned. Was it just the pregnancy or should she be taking vitamins or something? Had she had all the proper prenatal checks? Did she have backache? Headaches? Swelling feet? Had she suffered with morning sickness? He didn't like to think of her here alone struggling with the symptoms while he was away.

Not that he'd have been able to do anything useful. Janet had taught him that he wasn't much good in a sickroom. His mother had turned into a semi-invalid during her pregnancy with Emma and his bumbling efforts to help her hadn't been appreciated. Though he wasn't completely useless because he'd often looked after his baby sister. But the toddler had been easy to please, a joy to care for.

His heart squeezed uncomfortably. The urge to cherish Liz, wrap her in cotton wool, protect her, was incredibly strong. But maybe the protection she needed most was from him, from his past and his latent anger about those distant events.

Moving closer, he could see she'd been crying. Lashes clumped in spikes by moisture. A couple of wadded tissues sat on the bedside table.

The coward in him was tempted to tiptoe out, leave her to sleep longer. Quashing the impulse, he crouched beside her, his gaze following the delicate line of her jaw. With the back of his knuckle, he stroked the soft skin of her cheek gently until her eyes opened.

She rolled her head to look at him.

'Hey.' His voice was husky.

'Hey.' She regarded him solemnly.

'I'm sorry, Liz.' He took her hand, ran his thumb over the back of her long, slender fingers. 'I don't mean to hurt you.'

She sighed softly. 'I know.'

Her uncomplicated acceptance of his apology was a boon. She seemed sad, but she wasn't judging him. It was more than he deserved and her generosity freed him in an odd way. He traced the gold band of her wedding ring. 'No one's ever wanted to know about me, really know about me or my feelings, the way you do.'

'What about your grandmother?'

'Yeah, well, she did. In her way.' He squeezed her hand then released it as he stood up. Preparing to talk like this made him want to move, to pace, but there was nowhere to go. Holding himself still was an effort. He ran his hand around the back of his neck. 'Nanna was from a different generation. She was in her late seventies by the time I went to live with her permanently. By then I was thirteen with chips on both shoulders.'

'Thirteen? But…I thought your grandmother brought you up.' Her eyes were full of questions.

'I let you.' He rolled one shoulder, tilted his head, felt the tightness in his muscles. 'Nanna did her best for me when she could. When Janet and I lived with her on and off.'

'Janet?'

No wonder she sounded confused. He was making such a hash of this.

'My mother.' He turned, took a couple of steps to the window seat, subsided onto the cushion and pressed his fingers into the padded edge as he eyed Liz warily.

'You called your mother Janet?'

'She preferred it. I don't think she thought of herself as a mother.' He leaned forward, put his elbows on his thighs and clasped his hands. 'Maybe being called by her name made her feel less responsible.' He clenched his jaw then continued, 'I went to live with my grandmother after Janet died.'

There was a small silence. 'And she died when you were thirteen?'

He nodded once then looked down at his hands. A faint oil stain was still trapped in the crease of one thumb knuckle. He rubbed hard at it with the other thumb. 'From a drug overdose.'

'Jack—'

'I found her after school. But it was too late. That time.'

'That time?' Liz's voice wobbled but he couldn't look at her. 'It—it happened more than once?'

'Yes. Janet was an addict. She lived in the moment. If it felt good, she tried it.'

'Oh, Jack.' In his peripheral vision he saw Liz sit up and swing her feet off the bed. For a moment he was afraid she was going to come to him. If she touched him now, he'd disintegrate.

'Where was your father while all this was happening to you?' She sounded like she would cheerfully go into battle for him. His heart swelled, leaving his chest agonisingly full.

'I don't remember him. He was killed. Car accident. I was three.' His voice rasped out the short, stark sentences. But for the life of him he couldn't seem to form a nice flowing prose to soften the bald facts.

'Oh, Jack,' she said again. 'I'm sorry.'

'Yeah. Well.' He shrugged. This time he glanced at her in time to see a tear slip down her cheek. He tried for a reassuring smile, but his face was stiff and uncooperative. 'I didn't lack male roll models if that's what you're worried about. I had uncles.'

'U-uncles?' She swiped the moisture off her cheek.

'Whichever man Janet was involved with at the time. She thought having me call them uncle made us more like a family.' Now that he'd told her the worst, the words were coming more easily. But he'd still be glad when this was over. 'She never found anyone who was prepared to take on someone else's kid long-term.'

'That's what you meant this morning with that comment about uncles?'

'Yeah,' he said flatly. He glanced at her belly then met her eyes. 'I don't want that for any child of mine.'

'No. No, I can see that you wouldn't.' Her voice was little more than a whisper. She licked pale lips. 'Is this the reason why you don't want to have children? Because of the way your mother treated you? Because of the way the *uncles* treated you both?'

He nodded. 'Part of it.'

'But not all of it?' She looked at him shrewdly. 'You must see you would never be the sort of parent that your mother was, Jack. You have choices. You hate drugs. You never lose control. You are honourable and trustworthy and you never take the easy way out. That's not going to change.'

Her staunch support made him uncomfortable, almost claustrophobic.

'Perhaps I can come to you for a reference,' he quipped, hoping to lighten the atmosphere.

'Any time, any time at all.' She sounded as though she meant it. Her eyes were warm and expressive as they clung to his. 'Thank you for telling me this, Jack. I know how hard it was for you.'

'Yeah...well...' He fought the urge to squirm. She was thanking him and he'd only told her part of the story. Just like she'd said—he filtered the facts about his life, fed her titbits. He didn't want to keep her at a distance, but it was too much to expect him to be able to bare every single thing tonight.

He'd tell her...but for now it had to be enough that he'd made a start.

CHAPTER SIX

'DINNER will be ready.' Jack stood, feeling the relief flow through his body at the movement. He was strangely exhausted. Talking was damned hard work.

'Yes. It smells delicious.' Liz shifted, bracing herself to rise.

'Here.' He stepped to the edge of the bed, held out his hands and pulled her easily to her feet.

'Jack?' She stopped him from turning away with a hand on his forearm. The muscles that had eased with the end of their conversation suddenly tightened again as he waited. 'I'm sorry about some of the things I said last night.' She reached up with her other hand and cupped his jaw. The warmth seeped through to his heart. He missed her touch when her fingers dropped to her side after softly stroking down his cheek. 'You've always done more than your fair share of the cooking and I want you to know I appreciate it.' Her smile turned cheeky. 'Especially as you're so much better at it than I am.'

Relieved and embarrassed in equal parts, he gave a small grin. 'It's no hardship. I've always enjoyed it.'

'How did...?' The words trailed off as though she'd thought better of her question. Perhaps she sensed his reluctance to be drawn back into more revelations.

'How did I learn?' He could tell her that much. Turning his

arm, he captured her hand in his. 'One of the uncles was Italian. Used to cook enormous feasts. Nick was the only uncle I was sorry to see go. He was the one that lasted the longest.'

'What happened to him?'

He moved restlessly. 'He got tired of Janet's promises to stop the drugs so he left.'

'Leaving you with your...with Janet? On your own?'

'More or less.' Nick had been Emma's father and, for the three years he'd been around, the closest thing to a father that Jack had ever had. He could remember hoping the baby would mean that Nick would stay around. The exuberant Italian had been suing for the custody of his daughter when she'd died of meningitis. Too bad he hadn't been quicker. At least that would have been one less burden for Jack's conscience.

'Are you okay?'

He blinked, pulling himself out of his thoughts. Liz's eyes were searching his face, concern in the soft gold depths. Her beauty took his breath away.

'Jack?' A tiny frown formed on her face when he didn't answer. With her face tilted up to his, her mouth was in a perfect position for kissing. All he had to do was bend slightly, dip his head—

'Yes.' His voice was little more than a murmur. Her tongue flicked out to moisten her lips.

'Oh.' Liz's grip tightened with her sudden gasp, her strength almost vice-like. Alarmed, Jack reared back as she puffed small gasps of air, her eyes suddenly wide.

'What?' he demanded. 'What's wrong?'

'A contraction.' Puff. Puff.

'What?' Icy fingers clutched at his heart. 'You're delivering? I thought you weren't due for months.'

Liz's hold kept him still even though every instinct yelled for him to act, take charge. Do something *immediately*.

Except he had no idea what to do.

'No. No.' Puff, puff. 'It's a Braxton-Hicks. I—I didn't realise they could be so strong.'

'What the hell does it matter what it's called?' He took a deep breath. Yelling wasn't going to help. 'I'm taking you to hospital right now.'

'No. Wait a minute.'

An eternity later, she smiled at him. 'You can let go now.'

He looked down to where their hands were still linked, her fingers wriggling slightly in protest at his tight grasp. He chafed her hands, trying to rub away the red and white marks he'd left. 'Sorry. I'm sorry. I still think I should take you to the hospital for a check-up.'

'I'm fine now.' She retrieved one hand to rub her lower abdomen. 'And I've no intention of missing out on dinner.'

He frowned down at her. She was smiling as though nothing was wrong, as though she hadn't just given him the biggest bloody fright of his life.

'You're so damned small,' he said abruptly. 'How the hell are you going to give birth to a baby?'

'The way women have since the beginning of time.' She sounded so happy, so complacent about her ability that he wanted to shake her. 'I'm not giving birth in the middle of nowhere. The hospital's birthing unit has the best care in the world.'

'The best care in the world can't save you if the baby's too big. You should ask for a Caesarean.'

'I will not.' She looked up, her eyes dark with outrage. What was wrong with her? His suggestion was perfectly reasonable. 'I want to have a natural birth.'

'No.'

'Yes. Jack, this isn't all baby.' She patted the mound affectionately. 'There's a lot of amniotic fluid in here, too.'

'But you're only two-thirds through the pregnancy. Look

at the size of you already. And there's still how many more months to go? Three? The baby's going to be growing all that time.' He glared at her. 'Have you had tests?'

Her hands settled over her belly. 'Yes, I've had all the necessary tests. I told you this morning everything is proceeding just as it should be. There's no need to worry, Jack.'

'It's easy for you to say,' he muttered. 'You're a doctor. You've been through this before.'

'Not from this side I haven't.'

'Yeah, but you know what's going on.'

'Why are you so worried about this? There's no sign that there's going to be a problem.'

'But—' He stopped, swallowing the rest of his words. He couldn't dump his fears onto Liz when she seemed so full of confidence in her body, in her ability to do this enormous job. He'd never send a probie out into the field to fight a fire with a head filled with horror stories. How could he undermine Liz about this?

'But what? Jack?'

'Nothing.' He couldn't tell her about Janet's experiences with pregnancy. Or Kylie's. Besides, they were topics he wasn't ready to broach. 'Nothing. Just don't take any risks, okay?'

'I won't. I'm not.'

'No, of course not.' He ran a hand over his face, wishing he could wipe away his doubts.

'Why do I get the feeling I'm not really reaching you?' she said softly.

'You are. You are, Liz. Just…if the doctor tells you that you need a Caesarean, don't fight it. Promise me that much. Please.'

'I will, if it's necessary. But it won't be.'

'But I've got your promise?'

'Yes.'

'Good.' He nodded. 'Let's eat.'

* * *

The following week, Liz said goodbye to the last patient for the Saturday-morning clinic. Juggling a bundle of records on her hip, she turned to lock the office door.

'Should you be carrying those, Dr Campbell?'

'Jack!' She brought the folders around and clutched them to her chest, mortified to feel the rush of heat in her face. Her husband had caught her unawares and she was blushing? What was wrong with her?

'Hand them over.'

'What?' Her scattered wits fumbled to understand. 'Oh, the files? They're not heavy.'

'All the same.' He scooped them out of her arms. The sensation of his skin skimming across hers and then the briefest contact of his arm on her breast sent a swirl of excitement through her stomach. She suppressed a yelp and hoped he couldn't see how flummoxed she was.

'Where are you taking them?' he asked.

She looked at him blankly.

'The files.' With the stack balanced easily under his arm, he took her elbow. His fingers were warm on her bare flesh.

'B-back down to the main desk.'

'Lead on.'

She set off towards the lift, immediately missing his touch when his hand dropped from her arm. But at least her brain started functioning again.

'What are you doing here?' she asked.

'I've come to whisk you away from all this.'

'Have you?' Her footsteps slowed as she looked up into his eyes. Merriment twinkled in the blue depths. She couldn't help but be charmed by him. 'I'll come with you on the condition you're whisking me away to somewhere I won't have to move a muscle for twenty-four hours.'

'Tired?' His face creased in concern. 'Are you working too hard?'

'Yes, I am tired. And, no, I'm not working too hard.' Surreptitiously rubbing a twinge along her side, she turned into the lift corridor. 'You know, our maternal ancestors probably gathered berries all day and only stepped out of the briars to give birth.'

Jack pressed the down arrow then turned to look at her, his head cocked to one side. 'I hope that doesn't mean you intend to step out of the operating theatre to drop our baby in the hospital corridor.'

Amusement bubbled up at the picture his words painted. At the same time his easy use of *our baby* made her breath hitch. Did that mean he was coming to accept the thought of being a parent? Surely that was elation she was feeling… wasn't it? The odd brew of contrary emotion caught her by surprise. She pushed it aside to think about later.

'No, of course not.' She stepped into the lift and pressed the button for the lower floor. 'My point is that pregnancy is a normal function of the female body. I'm tired, not ill.' And she'd be a darned sight less tired if she could sleep properly. Insomnia plagued her with Jack sleeping in the spare room. But she wasn't going to tell him that. 'So where are you whisking me to?'

'Not far. I've got something to show you.'

'What is it?'

'Uh-uh, not telling. It's a surprise.' He ushered her out when the doors slid open. 'You'll like it. I promise.'

'I am tempted.' She sighed. 'But there's a mountain of washing waiting for me at home.'

'All done.' He grinned when she blinked at him. 'And don't worry, I colour co-ordinated. The whites are still white. It's drying as we speak. It'll be ready to bring in while you have a rest.'

'Mmm. A domesticated man. Every woman's favourite fantasy. You'll have my head filling with all sorts of ideas,' she teased.

'Really? What sort?' His voice lowered to a husky rumble and the world seemed to rock in response.

Her heart lurched into an alarming rhythm as she cast around for a safe response. 'How about you with a broom in one hand and a feather duster in the other?'

'Not quite what I'd envisaged,' he drawled.

She forced the muscles of her throat to swallow. For a fleeting moment she was tempted to say something that would deepen the unexpected intimacy. But she felt strangely shy, unable to take the step. They had so much still to work through.

And then there was the pregnancy. Her hand lifted of its own accord to smooth her baby bump. She loved her growing body, all the changes that were happening. But it was dramatically different from her trim pre-pregnancy self. The changes that so delighted her might turn him off. She wasn't ready to risk that level of exposure.

Liz walked the remaining distance to the main desk in tongue-tied silence.

'Hi, Hilda,' she said to the nurse on duty. 'We're returning this morning's clinic files.'

She stood aside so Jack could put them on the bench.

'Thanks, Liz. You're a dear.' Hilda winked at Jack. 'Enjoy the rest of your day.'

'We will. See you Monday.' Liz felt Jack's fingers stroke across the sensitive skin of her upper arm to close around her elbow again. 'S-so…where is this surprise of yours?'

'You'll see. Let's go.'

A few minutes later she was seated beside Jack in the four-wheel drive. Out of the corner of her eye she saw him turn to her. His hand rested on the edge of her seat. If she moved those few inches, she could lay her cheek on his fingers, invite his touch.

Suggest that he take her home…

And not to rest.

'Are you feeling up to this? Just say the word and I'll take you home.' His words dovetailed straight into her thoughts.

'I'm fine. Fine.' Liz straightened, grabbing the seat belt and pulling it across her body. If she got it shut fast enough, maybe it could somehow contain the treacherous images in her head. Her fingers fumbled on the catch then finally snicked it into place. 'Besides, I want to see this surprise you've promised.'

A short time later he turned into a nearly full car park. They were at Lake Dustin.

Liz bit her lip to stop herself from groaning aloud. Of all the places he could bring her while she was in danger of ambushing herself with unfulfillable lust...

Did he remember their first real kiss had been here? He'd spun her into his arms, his mouth capturing hers in an exquisite caress. She'd been as malleable as freshly wetted plaster of Paris in his hands. And just as hot. By the time he'd finished she hadn't needed to walk the rest of the lakeside track—she'd floated beside him in a daze. He could have seduced her that day—if he'd tried. But he'd been more subtle than that.

'I'll never make the walk around the lake,' she said as he opened the passenger door so she could climb out.

'I know.' The slow, wicked curve of his lips suggested that he remembered that kiss as well as she did. 'We're going to be very sedate, very...restrained today.'

She gulped in a breath and turned to pick up her handbag.

'Come on.' He dropped his arm around her waist and propelled her gently towards the gravel path. A small grey fantail darted and swooped in the shrubs to the side, completely unconcerned by their presence. 'I've booked for lunch.'

In the cosy little restaurant they were greeted by the waiter. He took them out to the lakeshore seating and left them with menus to peruse, promising to return soon for their order.

'Ah, perfect timing,' said Jack, when they were alone. 'Hear that?'

Liz became aware of a series of musical notes from across the water.

'It's our floor show. Look.' Jack pointed out to the island near the edge of the lake.

An elegant black swan stood at the waterline with three downy grey chicks.

'Oh, how gorgeous.'

'See Mama farther up the bank? That's her we can hear calling. She's chivvying junior to hurry up and join the rest of the family.'

Liz searched and soon spotted the second swan. Another grey fluff ball was struggling to navigate tangled growth. The slender black neck dipped and stretched as the adult swan continued her scolding.

'Tsk,' she said, smiling. 'There's always someone who needs that last-minute bathroom stop when everyone else is ready to go.'

With the group finally all together, the adults escorted their offspring ponderously to the lake. Once on the water, they glided regally across the surface.

Liz looked back at Jack to find him watching her, a small smile playing at the edges of his mouth.

'They mate for life. Swans.'

'Do they?' She could drown in the warm blue eyes that held hers. 'It's been a long time since you've shared any of these quirky little nature facts.'

'Yes, I guess it has.' He reached across to link his fingers with hers.

'I've missed it.'

'Have you?'

'Yes. Very much.'

'So have I.' He was silent for a moment, his finger rubbing

across the sensitive webbing at the base of her thumb. 'Liz, I—' He stopped, his gaze sliding past her. A muscle in his cheek twitched briefly.

'Hello, you two,' boomed a voice from close by. 'Fancy seeing you here.'

'Hello, Tony.' Jack's smile was friendly. Liz envied him his equanimity. She liked her boss, but his timing, in this instance, was dreadful.

Tony introduced his new girlfriend, then looked around at the now full tables. 'You were obviously sensible enough to book ahead.'

'Yes.' Jack managed to sound gently discouraging. Liz suppressed a sigh—if she knew Tony, the subtlety would be wasted.

'Mind if we join you?'

There was an expectant pause.

'Um, no, of…course not.' She looked at Jack helplessly.

'Great. Lucky we bumped into you. I've been wanting to try this place since it opened. It's had a terrific write-up in the local press.'

Liz smiled weakly as Jack signalled the waiter to arrange for the extra chairs.

She seesawed between irritation with herself and the urge to laugh. She desperately wanted to know what Jack had been going to say before the interruption. Whatever it had been, however small, it was important. Even if only because her close-mouthed husband was volunteering it.

CHAPTER SEVEN

THEY'D had three lovely weeks since Jack had told her about his parents, thought Liz as she watched open-day activity at the fire station. Two weeks since the lunch at the lake. Jack was still extraordinarily watchful of her. The days had fallen into a pattern. Almost like old times. Almost *better* than old times.

Except for two big things.

Their sleeping arrangements, for one. They were still in separate rooms. Trying to decide what to do about that caused her disproportionate angst so she resolutely refused to let her mind linger on the subject.

The other big thing was *her*. She blew out a small breath. How could two weeks make such a difference to the way she felt physically? She was waddling, slip-on shoes were a must. And thank goodness for the warmer days because she didn't need to wear pantyhose for work. The only problem was she really needed to make an appointment to have her legs waxed.

Not that Jack seemed inclined to look at them. The only thing he looked at was what she was doing and whether she was resting enough. She grimaced, aware her thoughts made her seem like a petulant child.

She didn't dare complain about how she was feeling. With Jack already worried about the delivery, he'd have her locked up in an operating theatre with an obstetrician stationed outside the door if she voiced even the smallest doubt. He put a good face on his concerns, but she could still sense them. Someone or something had affected him very deeply. His mother? Janet seemed the most likely source of his irrational fear.

Liz rubbed her back absent-mindedly. Had she done the right thing by not asking him to the prenatal classes? She'd wrestled with her conscience, but had convinced herself the classes would only give him more to worry about. A little bit of knowledge was dangerous.

But the trite saying wasn't giving her the comfort she'd managed to wring from it for the last fortnight. The truth was, knowledge was usually the best way to combat fear.

So now she had to squarely face the reason she didn't want him at the classes. Fear of her own vulnerability. Part of her longed to get closer to her husband, desperately wanted him to hold her, to tell her she was still desirable to him.

The other part wanted to keep some distance between them, to protect herself in case things didn't work out. Jack was making all the right sounds and he had broken down walls between them by opening up about his past. But there was still no guarantee he'd be able to take that next step to being an involved father.

Then there were the classes themselves. The intimacy between the couples was beautiful…but unnerving. Just the thought of sharing those moments with Jack was nearly enough to have her ready to spontaneously combust. Having him touch her hand or arm or back sent thrills racing up her spine these days. Imagine him at the classes with his hands on her belly, helping her do the exercises. Or rubbing her lower back, or her thighs.

She shut her eyes as a wave of heat engulfed her.

'Shouldn't you be sitting down?'

'Jack!' The heat flowed straight up to her face, threatening to scorch the skin with its intensity. 'You gave me a fright.'

'I'll give you more than that if you don't start being more sensible,' he growled, examining her closely. 'You're flushed. Have you been overdoing it?'

'No. Yes. Um, maybe I've had a little too much sun,' she said latching onto the idea, thankful that it would explain any redness in her face. Her lustful thoughts were nobody's business but her own.

'Hmm. I've got a talk to give the kids before lunch. Come and help me.' He reached for her hand. The action of his fingers slipping between hers focussed her feverish attention on the sensitive skin there. She couldn't have mustered an argument. 'That way I can keep an eye on you.'

She allowed herself to be towed into the fire station where thick matting on the concrete floor served as makeshift seating for a group of children. Parents sat in fold-up chairs at the back.

'Hi, kids,' said Jack, commanding their attention. 'Who's here for a fire safety talk?'

A chorus of enthusiastic replies greeted him.

'Fantastic. I'm Jack and this is my helper, Dr Liz. She's going to sit here.' He winked at her as he escorted her to a seat at the front. 'Right by the uniforms so she can help with buttons and things for those who want to dress up a bit later.'

For the next half an hour, Liz watched in amazement as Jack taught the children about fire safety and put them through their paces with practical exercises. He was so comfortable in the role that it couldn't be an act. She'd known in theory that part of his job before he'd gone overseas had been visiting local schools, talking to students. His lessons were given at their level of understanding. He wasn't talking down to them. And they were responding to him with obvious enjoyment.

She should be ecstatic about this unexpected side to him. So why wasn't she? What was wrong with her? Far from being reassured, she felt oddly bothered by it. If he was like this with his own child then he'd be a fantastic parent. Probably a better one than she would be. She frowned. She couldn't be competitive about this, could she? Her ambivalence was frightening.

At the end of the session the children were given the opportunity to dress up in firemen's uniforms and sit in the big pumper parked on the station's apron. Liz watched as Jack helped a girl of about six into a bright orange overall, chatting to her as he rolled up the excess material of the sleeves. He looked gorgeous in his dark blue uniform pants with the braces hooked over his shoulders. Liz's breath caught as he lifted the yellow helmet off his head. He set it at a jaunty angle on the girl's blonde curls before he hoisted the grinning child into the cabin with the other children. Liz found her lips curving spontaneously. Jack's smile, as he caught her eye, was brilliant.

She swallowed, blinking away the sudden tears that threatened. Hormones. It must be the pregnancy making her feel so strange. She turned her attention to a tot dragging a heavy jacket across the mat.

'You're very good with the kids,' she said a short time later when the crowd had dispersed. Even to her own ears it sounded more like an accusation than a commendation. She cleared her throat and tried to soften her tone. 'They like you.'

'Do you think so? Thanks. Ready for lunch, Dr Liz?' He grabbed her hand in a warm clasp. 'That barbecue is smelling pretty good to me.'

'Sure.' She let him lead her across to the shaded lawn, but food was the furthest thing from her mind. 'I didn't realise you'd spent much time around them.'

'Hmm?'

'Kids. I didn't realise you'd spent much time around children.'

'I took Monster Management 101 with Danny.' He slanted her a grin as they neared the barbecue. 'We go out to the schools quite often. You know that. How about I find you somewhere to sit and get lunch for both of us?'

'You never told me how much you enjoyed it.' His dismissal of this side of himself, as though it was nothing out of character, irritated her.

He stopped to look down at her, his forehead creasing into a frown. 'Are you mad with me, Liz?'

'No, of course not.' But she was for some reason, she realised as she fidgeted under his gaze.

'Jack! Liz!' a cheery voice hailed them. Liz looked past Jack to see Danny's wife, Sarah, waving at them from her spot under a sturdy old oak tree. 'Bring your lunch over here and sit with us. There's plenty of room.'

The odd moment of tension eased and Liz was glad to have an excuse to move away. Glad, too, that she didn't have to try to explain her attitude. How could she when she couldn't understand it herself?

Forcing her lips to smile, she waved back with her free hand. She started to move towards them, but Jack didn't release her immediately. She stopped, turning slightly to meet his eyes. His wry expression told her he knew she was running away from him rather than eager to socialise with their friends.

One corner of his mouth quirked. 'What a good idea,' he murmured. 'Why don't you join them? I'll get us something to eat. Do you want salad?'

'Yes. Please. Thanks.'

Sarah handed her a spare cushion as she reached the edge of the rug. Liz lowered herself and rested her back on the tree trunk beside Sarah and watched while Danny chased after his two-year-old daughter, Suzy.

'I'm going to have my work cut out for me once Suzy's brother arrives.' Sarah patted her stomach. 'She's a handful on her own.'

Liz smiled as she watched the child charging in the

opposite direction to her father. 'Don't you talk about my favourite toddler like that.'

'I should rent her out to you for a while so you can see what you're letting yourself in for.' Sarah sighed. 'She's running me ragged at the moment.'

Liz looked at her friend sharply, noting the circles under her eyes, the puffy hands and the way her sandal straps cut into her feet.

'How have you been feeling?'

'Are you asking as my friend or my doctor?'

'Both. But if you'll feel happier I'll put aside my Dr Liz hat for a few minutes.' Jack's nickname made her serious statement sound friendlier and not too intrusive.

'Dr Liz, huh?' Sarah smiled in appreciation.

'Jack's idea.'

'I like it. You must be pleased to have him back home.'

'Hmm.' Liz watched as her husband approached, balancing two laden plates and carrying the esky they'd dropped off earlier. 'Dr Liz wants to see you in her office early next week, okay?'

'All right.'

'Thank you.' She took the proffered meal from Jack. He dropped down beside her on the rug, propping himself on his elbow as he munched on a bread-covered sausage and onions.

'Will we see you at the antenatal class this week, Jack?' asked Sarah. 'It's a shame you couldn't get to the earlier ones. Understandable, though. With work. And jet-lag can leave you feeling like a limp rag for ages, can't it?'

Liz winced, chewing doggedly on a piece of meat that had suddenly turned to indigestible leather. So much for the benefits of lunching with friends.

'It sure can.' Jack gave her a bland look.

Encouraged, Sarah went on, 'I hope you'll be coming now you've recovered.'

Danny joined them a few minutes later with Suzy balanced on his shoulders. Liz hoped that might be enough to distract Sarah.

'I felt quite sorry for Liz, being the only one there on her own. You're not one of those men that thinks it's sissy to come to the classes, are you?'

'I—'

'Danny's coming even though it's our second, aren't you, darling?' Sarah patted his arm. 'It's good to have a refresher. Even Liz is there and she's a doctor—but as I explained to her when I talked her into coming to the classes, it helps to know what to expect afterwards as well. And you could do with the classes. You don't know anything about changing a nappy, do you?'

Liz stared as a strange spasm crossed Jack's face. *Did* he know about changing nappies? But how could he?

Luckily, Sarah didn't need any input from either of them as she swept on. 'Well, you don't want to be one of those men who doesn't have a clue, do you?'

'I certainly don't, do I?' he said benignly, raising an eyebrow at Liz. 'What night are these classes, Sarah?'

'Thursday.'

'Ah, Thursday. Silly me. I thought Liz had worked late that night.' His smile made Liz feel like a hapless mouse being toyed with by a particularly ferocious tomcat.

'I did. Work late.' She cleared her throat, the words seeming to stick on the way out. 'And, um, I went straight to the class because I knew you were tired.'

'Ah. Considerate of you. I'm glad you explained. It's good to have everything out in the open between us, isn't it, sweetheart? Especially at a time like this. Honesty is so important.'

'You know, you are so right, Jack,' gushed Sarah, missing the undercurrents and saving Liz from the necessity of answering him. 'I suppose you've done the basic delivery course, have you? Like Danny has through the emergency services? Still, when it's your own it's all a bit different.'

'Absolutely,' Jack purred. 'I'll definitely be there on Thursday. Liz will make sure. Won't you, darling?'

CHAPTER EIGHT

'WELL! Go on! Say it,' Liz said, as the silence in the vehicle stretched and took on a presence of its own.

'Say what?' Jack glanced at her briefly, then turned his attention to backing out of the parking space.

'That I should have told you about the damned classes.'

He slotted the stick into gear. 'I guess you had your reasons.'

'That's right. I did.' She folded her arms and tried to ignore the gymnastics happening in her belly. 'I'm not going to feel bad about this. *I'm not*. I made a decision. I weighed the evidence and I made a decision.'

'Not to tell me?'

'Yes.'

'Okay, then.'

'That's it? Just okay?' His easy acceptance stung. Didn't he think it was worth fighting for his rights as a father-to-be?

He sighed. 'What do you want me to say?'

'That you care, damn it. But you don't, do you?' *Shut up, shut up!* She knew he was doing the best he could, better than she'd expected him to do. She knew he was…but somehow her combative words seemed to have developed a momentum of their own. 'You don't want to come to the bloody classes because you don't care.'

'I haven't come to the bloody classes because I didn't know about them.'

'Well, now you do know about them.' She closed her eyes, hearing the gloating note in her voice. Her behaviour was appalling. How could she take back the things she'd said now? She was going to look like such an idiot.

An apology was starting to form in her mind when she heard him chuckling softly. She glared at him.

'What's so funny?'

'You know you're in the wrong. This *offence is the best defence strategy* isn't working.'

She sat rigidly mute, hating it that he'd reduced her righteous anger to little more than a tantrum. Never mind that she'd started to see her position as weak. That he had recognised the flaw was unbearable.

'You can't have this thing all ways, Liz.'

She wasn't ready to be jollied out of her mood. 'What do you mean?'

'You want me to be involved with the baby, you want me to bare my soul about my past. But you can't even bring yourself to tell me about the prenatal classes. How does that work? It doesn't sound fair to me.'

'I didn't want you to fuss more than you already are about the birth,' she said, trying to retrieve the ground she'd lost. 'And besides, I didn't think you would want to come.'

'How do you know if you don't give me the chance?'

He was right. He was right. But... 'But the bottom line is that you don't want children so why would you want to come to the class?'

He shook his head slightly as he pulled into their driveway. 'Low blow, Liz. I'm here, aren't I? The fact is I'm going to be a father. What I want or don't want is irrelevant now.'

'But it's not irrelevant to me.' The last thing she wanted to hear was this philosophical acceptance of his position. 'I want my baby to have an involved father. Not some distant man who wafts in and out of the house.'

He switched off the ignition and the silence settled around them. Turning towards her, he laid his arm along the back of the seat. 'I'll be as involved as you'll let me be, Liz.'

'Oh, that's right. Put it all back onto me,' she cried. 'If you're so interested, how come you haven't even asked whether we're having a boy or a girl?'

'Probably because I'm a man and the finer points of this sort of thing elude me.' He sighed, rubbing his forehead as though trying to ease tension there. 'So, what is it?'

'What?'

'The baby. Is it a boy or a girl?'

'Yes.' She released her seat belt and gathered up her bag, clutching it in front of her as she glared at him. 'Yes. It *is* a boy or a girl.'

His narrowed eyes examined her face as though seeking a clue to her meaning. 'Liz, sweetheart, you're not making sense.'

'I'm pregnant, Jack.' She let herself out of the car and turned back to look at him. 'I don't have to make sense.'

The satisfaction of slamming the car door sustained her all the way onto the veranda where she realised she didn't have a house key. By the time she thought of the one in the pot-belly, Jack had joined her. She maintained a dignified silence while he unlocked the door and opened it for her.

'Thank you.'

'No problem.'

'I—I'm going to lie down.'

'Good idea.'

In the bedroom, she subsided onto the edge of the bed and let her bag slip to the floor. She felt lonely and guilty and miserable. Weak tears seeped out as she lay down, curling around her now quiet belly. Not even the baby wanted to communicate with her.

If she kept pushing Jack, their marriage would have no chance. He'd leave and her baby would be deprived of a full-time father. Is that what she wanted? She'd psyched herself into going it alone while he'd been away. But it was different now, a little voice whispered. She'd started to hope things might work out. With hope came the possibility of being let down. If she kept behaving like she had today, that disappointment was a certainty.

She woke with a start to the raucous notes of a kookaburra's laugh. A quick glance at the clock told her she'd only slept for about half an hour, but she felt refreshed.

Jack. The memory of their argument flooded back, a faithful replay of every irrational moment driving her out of her relaxed state. She needed to talk to him, apologise and hopefully explain her position. Which might be tricky since she didn't understand it herself. But the important thing was the apology.

She splashed water on her face and tidied her hair, dragging it back into the band. She studied herself in the mirror. The nap had wiped away most traces of her tears, but her eyes still had puffy circles beneath them.

Did Jack really mean he'd come to the classes or had he just said that to get Sarah off his back? No, that wasn't fair. He wasn't in the habit of saying things for expedience.

Oh, God. If he came to the class, how was she going to cope? He'd have to touch her. As things were, she was aware of him, his body, *all the time.* Sleeping on her own while he'd been away was a completely different proposition to sleeping alone when he was in the house…just down the hallway. Did he toss and turn at night, rumple the sheets?

She brought her thoughts back to the class. Would it be the catalyst that ripped away the fragile peace that they'd established these last few weeks?

She grimaced at her reflection. Perhaps she'd find out first-hand if spontaneous combustion really happened. Putting off the moment wasn't going to make it any easier.

It took a few minutes before she realised he wasn't around. In the kitchen, she found a short note. Blast. He'd gone back to the station. Her apology was practically burning on her lips—the least he could do was be around so she could deliver it. She touched the strong, flowing script, her mind churning.

Did this mean he was going to start using the station as a means of escaping difficulties between them again? She didn't want them to drift back to that. And she was the one in the wrong over this so she was the one who needed to make the first move.

Before she could change her mind, she scooped her keys off the bench and went to get her bag.

Jack threw the last of the empty bottles into the recycling bin and wheeled it out to the kerb for the next day's council collection.

He walked slowly back to the four-wheel drive, pulled a twig out of the grill, kicked the front tyre. Perhaps he should check the tyre pressures while he was here…or perhaps he should just stop putting off the inevitable. He had to go home some time.

But he didn't want to while things were so tense with Liz. Why hadn't she told him about the prenatal classes? Her secretiveness confused him, hurt him more than he'd have believed possible. On one hand she demanded he be involved, on the other she seemed to be blocking him out. He couldn't understand what was going on. What more could he do? He was here, wasn't he?

Jiggling the keys in his pocket, he wandered along to the back tyre to stare at it moodily.

He was trying, wasn't he? Hadn't he bared his soul about his past? Some of the important things anyway. Why couldn't Liz appreciate that it wasn't easy for him? A bit of trust would be nice. He thought whipping up his aggrieved feelings might help him suppress the inconvenient memory of the things he hadn't told her. It was too much to expect him to have blurted out everything at once. It wasn't that he *wouldn't* tell her about Emma and Kylie, it was just that he hadn't…*yet*.

As he reached for the vehicle's door handle, a yell from the house across the road brought him up short. A moment later came a clattering bang. Danny? Jack began to run, his heart in his mouth. He knew his friend had gone home to clean out the roof guttering.

He was halfway across the bitumen when Liz's car turned into the road. Without breaking stride, he signalled to her, hoping she'd realise something was amiss.

He met Sarah running back along the side path towards the fire station.

'Jack! Thank God you're still here. Danny…' She gulped. 'Oh, God! The ladder. I can't move it. He's—he's—'

'Sarah!' He held her by the shoulders, speaking sharply. 'I'll help Danny. Liz is just pulling up in the car. Go out and tell her to bring her bag in. Okay?'

She focussed on him after a moment then nodded.

'Go on now. I'll look after Danny.' He left at a run, dreading what he would find. It was almost comic relief to find his friend conscious and swearing a blue streak.

'Jack. Can you get this bloody thing off me?' A metal ladder pinned him to the collapsed remains of a plastic table.

'Hold still, mate.' Jack lifted the heavy appliance aside. 'Don't try to move. Liz is on her way.'

'I'm fine. Fine,' he gasped. 'Winded. That's all. Give us a hand up, will you?'

'Better to get you checked over.' Jack put out a restraining hand. 'Liz will be here in a sec.'

And then she was dropping to her knees on the other side of Danny.

'Hey, Danny. Jack's right. We need you to keep still while

we check you over.' Her lips curved in a reassuring smile, her voice having just the right note of caring and command to have the lanky fireman's grumbles tailing off. 'Sarah tells me you fell off the ladder.'

'Yeah. She'd just told me to move the bloody thing, too.' He grimaced. 'Suppose she'll be saying she told me so.'

'Guaranteed, hotshot,' Sarah's voice piped up, the jaunty words betrayed by the wobble of fear in her voice. 'As soon as you're back on your feet.'

'Have you got any pain?'

'More of an all-over bruised feeling. Like I've fallen off a ladder and had the damned thing land on me,' he joked.

'Did you hit your head?'

'Yeah. But I don't think that'll cause me any problems.' He smiled. 'Don't you have to have a brain for that? Seriously, I don't think I've hurt myself at all, Liz. I'm bloody lucky.'

'Looks like it. But since I'm here I may as well give you the once-over.'

'Gimme a break.'

'Good practice for me.' She smiled, obviously not about to be deflected as she reached for his wrist.

Jack grinned inwardly. Danny might as well lie back and let himself be cared for—his feeble protests weren't going to sway Liz once she'd made up her mind.

'I want you to tell me if you have any pain where I touch you.'

Danny produced a strained chuckle. 'Should you be doing this while my wife's watching?'

'You're safe. I'm a professional, tough guy,' Liz said, grinning.

Jack watched her long clever fingers work her patient over thoroughly from top to toe. After attaching a cervical collar, she organised him and Sarah to help turn Danny so she could check his back.

'This is embarrassing,' grumbled Danny.

'Never mind. Embarrassment never killed anyone,' Liz said in a matter-of-fact tone. 'Blood pressure, and then we'll think about letting you up.'

'Sarah, love. I'm sorry for being such an idiot.'

'You make sure you listen to me in future,' Danny's wife scolded.

'I promise I—' Danny stopped on a groan.

'Danny. What's happening?'

'Stabbing pain. Chest.'

'Just started?' Liz reached for his wrist, felt the rapid pulse, noted the short, gasping breaths. 'Pain anywhere else, Danny?'

'Right. Arm.'

'Oh, God. Liz?' gasped Sarah. 'Is he having a heart attack?'

'No, it's his lung. Sarah, sweetie, have you called the ambulance? Could you go and do that for me now?' Liz said, keeping her voice level, reassuring. 'Jack, can you get me a chest kit from the car? In the boot, left-hand side, clearly marked.'

A slight bluish tinge was already starting to form around Danny's lips.

Using the scissors from her bag, she snipped up the seam of his T-shirt then grabbed her stethoscope. She closed her eyes and listened intently. Breath sounds were markedly decreased on the right side. A quick tap on his ribs gave the resonance she was expecting.

'Danny, your lung has collapsed. I need to put a tube in to help it reinflate.' She prepared a large-gauge needle and syringe in case she had to resort to emergency measures. He hadn't deteriorated to a tension pneumothorax, but she wanted to be prepared to act quickly if it did. Much better if she could take the extra minutes to insert a chest tube, though.

'Whatever. You need. To do,' he gasped.

'Okay, I'm giving you a local anaesthetic. You'll feel a sting.' She injected him over the lower rib then swabbed the area liberally with iodine solution.

Jack knelt beside her the kit in his hands. 'What can I do?'

She opened a pack of green sterile drapes.

'I'll need one tube and a haemostat. That's the blunt-nosed clamp with scissor handles. I'll need that first.' She snapped on a pair of surgical gloves and positioned the drapes over Danny's ribs. 'See at the top there's the two layers? Can you hold it and peel open the covering when I tell you?'

'Okay.' In her peripheral vision she could see him getting the packages ready.

'Can you feel this, Danny?' She touched the scalpel to his skin.

'Just. Pressure.'

'Great. Hold still for me now.' She made a small incision along the rib.

'Jack, I need the haemostat. Yep, that's it. It's sterile so be careful not to touch it.' She slotted her fingers in the handles. 'Can you get the tube ready to open, please?'

She pushed the blunt nose into the cut, up and over the rib, through the cartilage, felt the small give as it entered the chest cavity.

'Okay, Jack. Ready for you to open, please. Thanks,' she said as she grasped the end of the tube with the blood-stained clamp. Pushing gently but firmly, she threaded it through the incision into the lung space.

'Okay, Danny. You should start to notice a difference in a minute.' She checked the one-way valve on the tube before taping a dressing into place over the wound.

The sphygmomanometer cuff was still in place around Danny's arm. She reinflated it and took another reading. There'd been a drop in his blood pressure, but it wasn't dangerously low. She'd check again in a minute, make sure it was coming back up.

Danny blew out a breath as she picked up his wrist. 'Thanks, Liz.'

'My pleasure, Danny.' She smiled at him. His pulse was

stabilising and his breathing had definitely eased. 'I think you'd better stay off ladders for a while, though.'

'He will be,' said Sarah, coming back to kneel at his side, sniffling back her sobs when she saw he was all right. 'The ambulance is on its way, Liz.'

'Well done, Sarah.' With her fingers still on Danny's radial pulse, Liz studied the younger woman's pale, puffy face. 'Is Suzy asleep?'

'No. I'd not long put her down. The noise must have woken her. She's playing in her cot.' A look of dismay crossed Sarah's face as she put a hand on her stomach. 'Oh, dear. I wanted to go to the hospital with Danny.'

'There's no reason why you can't.'

'But I can't think who to ask to mind Suzy. Normally I'd ask Debbie, but she's away.' Her voice tailed off as her face began to crumple.

'I've got a better idea.' Liz squeezed Sarah's shoulder. 'Why don't you pack a bag for you and Suzy? And both of you can come into the hospital with Danny. We'll fix you up a family room for the night. I know the management so I can pull some strings for you,' she teased. 'Not quite five-star accommodation, but the staff are very nice.'

Sarah gave a small hiccuping laugh, some of the tension easing from her face. 'Oh, Liz. Could you?'

'I'd prefer you weren't out here on your own. Besides, I have an ulterior motive. This way I can check your blood pressure and be sure you're getting some rest.' Liz's lips twitched. Jack's words coming out of her own mouth. She lifted her gaze to find him looking straight at her. Her pulse spiked. Phew, perhaps she should check obs on herself.

'It'll be through the roof at the moment,' Sarah said.

Liz took a moment to make the connection. 'Oh, yes. Your blood pressure. After Danny's acrobatics.'

'Sorry, love.' Danny sounded sheepish as he reached out for Sarah's hand.

Liz felt like a voyeur, witnessing the loving glance that passed between them.

A siren wailed in the distance. 'There's the ambulance, Sarah. How about getting that bag organised?'

'I'll let the ambos know where we are,' said Jack, leaving her alone with her patient.

'Thanks for looking out for Sarah, Liz,' Danny said when his wife had gone.

'My pleasure.' Liz began measuring his vital signs again. 'You'll both rest easier if you don't have to worry about each other.'

'Yeah. So am I going to live, Doc?' Danny smiled tiredly.

'I think you will if Sarah takes your ladder away.' Liz deflated the cuff, pleased with his progress.

He chuckled. 'Thanks. I thought I was done for. How soon do you reckon I'll be back at work?'

'We need to see how your lung stabilises over the next twenty-four to forty-eight hours.' Out of the corner of her eye Liz could see Jack returning. His booted feet stopped beside her.

'And speaking as your new boss, you won't be back at work until your doctor gives you the all-clear. However long that takes.'

Two paramedics rolled a gurney along the patio towards them.

After the four of them had transferred Danny, Liz tried to get up. Her legs were powerless, the joints locked into position. She felt awkward, ungainly. How embarrassing. She began to rock slightly to see if that would help to get one of her feet under her.

'I've got you.' Jack's voice, soft and close behind her as the trolley moved away.

A moment later he grasped her under her arms and pulled

to her feet. She expected him to release her immediately. Instead, his hands slid down to her hips. Her knees trembled, threatened to give way. He must have felt her unsteadiness because one hand slid between her belly and her breasts and his arm braced her. Suddenly his torso was pressed against her back. She could feel the solid heat of him through her flimsy top. Her heart hammered against her sternum and she wondered if he could feel the frantic beat.

'Are you all right?' His voice was low and gravelly.

'Yes. Thanks,' she said breathlessly.

But still he didn't release her. His fingers splayed across her ribs beneath her arm, his grip sure and strong. Her skin quivered, wanting, needing.

If she moved his hand to her breast, would his fingers mould to her curves? Oh, God. The thought made her weak with desperation for more of his touch.

She turned slightly to look up into his face. His blue eyes were dark and brooding. His mouth hovered above hers. If he bent his head just a little, his lips would mesh with hers. She felt herself sag back into him, her eyelids half closing as a tiny helpless whimper escaped.

'Am I hurting you?' His other hand curled around the nape of her neck, sending a thrill across sensitive nerves to shiver through her body.

'No,' she whispered, her eyes glued to his, willing him to turn her, to hold her. To kiss her.

Seconds stretched. Abruptly she realised she could hear the clatter of the gurney being loaded into the ambulance. Disconnected thoughts rushed in. The ambulance! Danny! Sarah!

She leapt away from Jack. The action nearly unbalanced her again. His hand shot out to steady her.

Thank goodness the noise had bought her to her senses. In another few moments she'd have taken matters into her own hands and tugged Jack's mouth down to hers.

'You coming, Liz?' One of the paramedics stuck his head around the end of the house.

'Yes, I'll be right there.' Liz bent to pick up her bag, but Jack was there before her. She felt the heat rush to her face as she tightened her fingers around the proffered handle. His expression was inscrutable when she met his eyes. He obviously hadn't been as affected by that brief, intense contact as she had been. She swallowed hard, struggling to collect her thoughts. 'Will you bring Sarah and Suzy up to the hospital, please?'

He nodded.

'Thanks. I'll see you there, then.' She turned and walked away on trembling legs.

CHAPTER NINE

By THE time Liz had Danny taken along to the X-ray department, Jack had arrived with Sarah and Suzy. He had the toddler balanced easily on one hip, her precious orange walrus dangling from his hand. The image he made with the child in his arms was gorgeous…and, in an odd way, threatening by the very naturalness of it. He didn't look at all like a man who didn't want children.

Liz dragged her eyes away and noticed Sarah's bag swinging from his other hand. Glad to have something concrete to focus her attention on, she signalled an orderly and arranged for the suitcase to be taken through to Danny's room.

She turned back to Jack. 'You'll be all right to look after Suzy while Sarah and I have a talk, won't you?'

She heard the words coming out of her mouth, felt the sharp look Hilda, the duty nurse, gave her. What was she doing? Hadn't she just gone to a great deal of trouble to wangle a sitter for Suzy?

'Sure.' Jack's quizzical look made her wonder if he realised her abrupt change of plans.

'There's, um, a box of toys in the corner.' Perhaps asking him to look after Suzy was inspired thinking. But Liz's innate honesty wouldn't allow her the comfort of dissembling. Was she setting him up, hoping he'd fail? Why would she do that?

Shouldn't she want him to have good experiences with children so he'd embrace his own? She shoved the thought aside for later. Right now she had things to do. 'If you have any problems, um, Hilda's on the front desk. She'll help you out.'

Liz sent a pleading look Hilda's way and was given a well-deserved disapproving one in return. Resigned to having to explain her behaviour later, Liz picked up Sarah's chart and pinned a determined smile on her face.

'Let's go through to a cubicle, Sarah,' she said, indicating the way. 'Hop on the scales for me first and then we'll get you up on the bed.'

'Oh, no,' Sarah protested good-naturedly. 'I knew I shouldn't have had that extra chop at the barbecue today.'

'Have you noticed any sudden weight gain since I saw you last?' Liz jotted the weight down, noting how it had jumped since Sarah's last appointment six weeks ago.

'Yes, I feel like an elephant. Much worse than I was with Suzy. But Mum said it was the same for her after her first pregnancy.'

'You've got quite a bit of puffiness, too. Did that start about the same time, can you remember?' Liz looked critically at her friend, taking stock of her rather swollen hands and face. A quick glance at her feet showed they were worse, with the sandal straps cutting into oedematous flesh.

'Isn't that just because I'm drinking so much water with these hot days we've been having? I'm always a bit like this in summer anyway. And Mum said it was normal in pregnancy.'

'Your mum's right, a little bit of oedema certainly can be normal. But it can also be a symptom of an underlying problem.' Liz picked up a small yellow-topped specimen jar from the shelf. 'Feel like giving me a urine sample?'

'Always.' Sarah pulled a face as she took the proffered container. 'Don't you have the same problem?'

'Absolutely.' Liz smiled sympathetically. 'Some days, my bladder rules my life.'

When Sarah came back, Liz helped her up on the bed and chatted while she tested the fluid sample with a dipstick. She frowned as the pale green square turned darker. A two-plus reading for protein. Not a good sign. She discarded the stick in the biohazard bin.

'Jack's a dark horse, isn't he, Liz? Suzy doesn't usually like strangers. Not that Jack's a stranger, but he's never made a huge fuss over her or anything so she's not all that familiar with him. But she was really happy for him to carry her and Wally. Which made things so much easier for me. He's going to be a great dad.'

'Hmm.' Liz's stomach gave an odd little swoop as she fumbled to secure the sphygmomanometer cuff on Sarah's arm. Luckily her friend chatted on happily, not needing an answer.

Liz released the air valve and took the readings as the mercury fell on the gauge.

'Had any headaches, Sarah? Nausea? Visual disturbances?'

'Nothing out of the ordinary. I've seen stars a couple of times when I got up too quickly.' Sarah frowned. 'Why? Is something wrong?'

'Your blood pressure is higher than it should be.' Liz looped her stethoscope around her neck. 'One hundred and fifty over ninety-two.'

'But that's only because of Danny, isn't it? I mean, he gave me an awful fright.'

'The stress of his accident might be a contributing factor, but you also have protein in your urine, which tells me that your kidneys aren't functioning as well as they should be. I want to run some more tests, but for now I want you on pretty strict bed rest to see how your blood pressure settles. I'd like to keep you in hospital for observation for a day or two.'

'A day off my feet would be bliss.'

'It might be longer than that, Sarah. I'm concerned that you're showing symptoms of pre-eclampsia. We should take extra precautions immediately rather than wait for the tests to confirm it.'

'I feel fine, though. Wouldn't I feel sick if there was something really wrong?'

'Not always. It can be insidious.'

'Surely it's not that bad. What if I promised to take it easy?'

'You're not going to be able to get the rest you need if you're running around after an active two-year-old.'

Sarah stared, her dismay obvious. 'But what will I do about Suzy? And Danny, now that he's hurt himself? Mum's not coming for another fortnight.'

'Do you think she'd be able to come sooner?'

'Liz! You're really scaring me.'

'Sarah, pre-eclampsia is a serious condition if it's not treated properly. We'll run some more tests. But if you do have it, and I think it's highly likely, we've caught you early. With care we should be able to stop it from progressing.' Liz laid a hand on her friend's shoulder. 'It's important that we get control of this. For your sake and for the sake of the baby.'

'The baby? I'm not going to lose the baby, am I?'

'No, not if we take steps now.' Liz knew she shouldn't give such a definitive answer, but with Sarah's eyes pleading with hers, with her own pregnancy nearing the same stage, she was powerless to resist giving the reassurance. 'You're thirty-four weeks. Even if we had to deliver you right this minute your baby would have a great chance. But it will be even better if we can keep him where he is for another three weeks. So, how about it? Will you do the bed rest?'

'Yes. Absolutely. Just try to get me off it.'

'Good girl.' Liz chuckled. 'We will let you do a bit of gentle exercise, but mostly bed rest until I've done a consult with one of the Melbourne Women's OB specialists. I'll find out what monitoring we can do for the baby to make sure everything's the best it can be. Now, let's get you along to Dustin Base Hospital's brand-new family room. We'll discuss with Danny how we're going to manage this before we settle Suzy in with you.' She checked her watch. 'His chest X-ray should be back by now as well.'

'I'll get Jack to bring Suzy through now,' said Liz after she'd finished talking to Sarah and Danny. 'I want you to ring for assistance if she needs anything. Anything at all. The nurses will pop in to feed her and to check on her through the evening. I don't want either of you out of bed except to visit the bathroom for twenty-four hours. Got it?'

'Yes, ma'am,' they chorused in unison.

'That's what I like, well-behaved patients.' Liz grinned, hooking Sarah's chart onto the foot of the bed. 'I'll come and say goodnight before I leave.'

Her mind on the phone call she needed to make to the obstetrics specialist, Liz strode purposefully along the corridor. When she turned into the waiting room, her steps faltered. Jack was slouched comfortably in a chair, his feet resting on the low table, his long legs bent to form a saddle for Suzy who sprawled on his stomach, fast asleep. One hand rested across the toddler's back, fingers splayed to hold her securely in position.

The poignant picture pierced straight to Liz's heart, bringing a painful lump to her throat and quick moisture to her eyes. Fortunately, Jack hadn't noticed her arrival with his attention focussed on the magazine he held in his other hand. She took two careful steps in reverse and leaned her trembling frame back against the wall outside the room.

Today had presented such astounding revelations about her husband. She struggled to balance them against the reality that she'd thought she knew. Who was he really? The man who didn't want a family but was prepared to do his duty by his pregnant wife? Or the man who handled groups of children with consummate ease all day then stepped up in an emergency to gently cradle the slumbering toddler of friends?

Intellectually, she knew which she wanted him to be. But why was her spirit so disturbed when he slotted so perfectly into that role?

She bent her head to massage her temple with stiff fingers, feeling the tension there begin to ease slightly. If only she could massage the turmoil out of her beleaguered mind as simply.

'Liz? Everything all right?'

She jolted out of her reverie to see Hilda looking at her with concern.

'Oh, yes.' Liz could hear the husky wobble in her voice. 'Just, um, reviewing, um, some treatment to make sure I hadn't missed something.' She straightened away from the wall and continued brightly, 'Well, I'd better get on.'

She could feel Hilda's eyes lingering on her as she took a few seconds to compose herself before facing Jack. She fiddled with her white coat, checking the lapels, adjusting her stethoscope while she took a deep breath. In. And out. Fixing a smile onto her face, she walked back into the room to find Jack sitting up, watching the door expectantly.

She stopped, her fragile poise fracturing as her eyes met his.

'Problems?' He arched one brow.

'No. No. Um.' She swallowed and tried to gather her thoughts. 'Would you be able to take Suzy along to the room now? I'll get someone to come down in a few minutes to give her dinner. And, um, I need to make a phone call before we can go home.'

'Sure.'

Before he could say more Liz was gone, leaving only the memory of her stricken face. Jack sighed, feeling suddenly tired. She was confusing him. One minute she was open and approachable, the next so prickly and cold that he didn't know whether to advance or retreat. With the way her eyes darted away every time he caught her gaze, he was beginning to get the feeling that she couldn't bear the sight of him.

And she'd looked so ill at ease just now. A far cry from the calm, competent professional who'd acted without hesitation to save Danny's life a couple of hours ago.

When he'd helped her up after the paramedics had taken Danny to the ambulance, she'd been so soft and warm as he'd held her against his chest to steady her. Her dark hazel eyes had clung to his, almost seeming to invite his kiss for those precious seconds before they'd been interrupted. The timing had been appalling and a moment later she was moving away, the opportunity lost. Too late now to wish he'd gone with his first crazy impulse to swoop on her slightly parted lips. Her response, or lack of it, might have answered at least one of the questions swirling in his mind.

He tossed the magazine back onto the table and shifted Suzy's weight in his arms. The toddler murmured a sleepy protest as he got to his feet. His lips curved as he looked down at her. She was so relaxed she seemed boneless. Just the way Emma used to lie in his arms all those years ago, so innocent, so trusting. His heart swelled with the memory.

In just under three months it would be his own child he'd be holding in his arms. He never wanted his child to feel the destructive fear and uncertainty he'd felt while he was growing up.

Safety and security. That's what children needed. They needed to know the adults in their life would do the right thing, or make a damned good attempt to.

Whatever happened between him and Liz, they had to make sure they did the right thing as parents.

He looked down into Suzy's untroubled face and suddenly realised how fiercely he wanted to be there for his child. Not just a part-time father at weekends. He wanted it all. And he wanted Liz in his life, in his bed. In his heart. He firmed his resolve. He was prepared to wait, but he wasn't prepared to let go.

He smiled grimly. *Look out, darlin'*, he warned his wife silently. *Things are going to change around here.*

* * *

Later, Jack walked through to the lounge at home with two cups of freshly-brewed green tea.

'You—'

'I—' Liz accepted one of the drinks. 'Sorry, Jack, what were you going to say?'

He grinned at her, appreciating the picture she made with her glossy dark hair now loosely curling over her shoulders. She seemed to be glowing with good health. Pregnancy obviously suited her. 'Always the way, isn't it? Nothing to say since we left the hospital and now we both want to talk at the same time.'

'Hmm.' She looked into her drink as though she might see the answers to the world's mysteries there.

Refusing to be put off by her lukewarm response, he sat on the two-seater couch beside her, resting his arm along the back and curving his body towards her. He smiled mentally at the brief, wary glance she shot him from the corner of her eye. 'I was going to say that I thought you were fantastic today.'

That got her attention. Her head came round and troubled hazel eyes met his.

'What do you mean?'

'With Danny.' He reached out to tuck behind her ear a strand of hair that had curled across her cheek. Her eyes darkened briefly before she looked away.

'Oh, that.'

'You saved his life today,' he said softly.

She shrugged. 'It's my job.'

'Yes, it is. All the same, I enjoyed watching you work. I saw how quickly he went down. One minute he was great and the next…' He grimaced. 'If we'd had to call the ambulance and wait for them to arrive, I don't think he'd have made it. Because you were there he got the treatment he needed when he needed it.'

After a small pause he said, 'Which reminds, why were you there?'

Because his eyes were still on her, he saw her almost imperceptible start.

'Oh. Um, I—I wanted to talk to you. And—and I wasn't sure how long you were going to be at the station.'

'It must have been important,' he said, keeping his voice gentle, undemanding.

She bit her lip then took a quick sip from her cup. 'It *seemed* important at the time.'

Whatever she'd wanted to discuss, she obviously wanted to avoid it now.

'So, talk to me,' he invited, resisting the temptation to touch her again in case it distracted her.

Her breasts rose as she took a deep breath.

'I owe you an apology.' The words seemed to rush out. 'For not telling you about the prenatal class. It wasn't fair for you to find out that way from Sarah. And…and I'm sorry for the other stuff.'

'Other stuff?'

'Leaving you with Suzy at the hospital, for a start. Not that you didn't cope brilliantly. And, um, I'm sorry for the other things that I said to you earlier.'

'That's okay.'

'No, Jack.' She looked at him fiercely. Now that she'd made the commitment to speak she seemed determined to see it through. 'It's not okay.'

He shrugged, struggling to maintain a passive exterior while inside he was rejoicing. 'You must have had your reasons.'

'Maybe I did. But they're not reasons I'm proud of. And I've realised that you're right, I can't have it both ways.' She took another quick drink. 'Do you want to come to the classes?'

'Do you want me to?'

'I don't know,' she said after a few moments, turning to him with an anguished expression. 'Yes. And no. I feel so contrary. Oh, God. I don't know what I want.'

His heart went out to her. He didn't understand why the classes were a problem, but his instinct was to try to make it easier for her. 'Would you prefer me not to come to the classes?'

'It's not that. It's just the classes are so…' She looked away again. He watched her throat move as she swallowed. 'So, um, hands on.'

'Hands on?' The implication dropped into his mind, sent his mood into a dive. Where were they going to go from here if she couldn't bear him near her? 'As in *actually* hands on?'

'Yes.' She stared at her cup, picking at the design on the front with her thumbnail.

'I see.' He digested her words, absorbed the hurt. 'And you don't want me touching you.'

'Oh, no!' Her head came up and she looked at him. 'It's not that.' The spontaneous denial lifted his suffocating gloom.

She shrugged. 'I mean, I'd like you to come to the class, um, you know, if you want to, that is. I just want you to know you don't have to. If you don't want to.'

'Good,' he said. His mood swung even higher, but he ruthlessly subdued his exultation. He didn't want to spook her now. 'That's settled. I'm coming.'

'I'll understand if you can't make it, though. If you've got to work or something.'

'I'll be there.'

'Okay.' She sipped her tea, a small frown pleating her forehead.

'These classes are to learn about the baby?'

'Yes. And to learn exercises to make the delivery easier, techniques to manage the pain.'

'Surely they give you drugs for that. Don't they do epidurals or something these days?'

'Not necessarily. I told you I want a natural birth.'

He opened his mouth to argue, but managed to swallow the words before they emerged. He had plenty of time before the due date, surely he could talk her out of doing it tough before then. The last thing he wanted right now was to spoil their truce.

'The other thing the classes teach us is what to expect at the delivery. I mean, I know what's going to happen, of course, but I've never been on this side of the process before. Obviously. But it's for the husbands who are going to attend the delivery as well so they know what will happen.' She looked at him expectantly.

'Right.' He could see instantly that wasn't the response she was after.

The corners of her mouth crimped briefly.

'Well, are you going to come to the delivery?'

'Yes.'

'Because if—' She stopped, a startled look on her face. Her mouth opened and closed as though she was having trouble finding a response. 'Oh. Well. All right, then.'

'So are we having a boy or a girl?'

He looked down to where her hand curled over her stomach in a protective gesture. 'A girl.'

The rush of primitive emotion that surged through him was a shock. Knowing the sex made the baby even more real. He was going to have a daughter. A *daughter*.

'Jack?'

He glanced up to find her eyes searching his face.

'Are you disappointed?'

'No. Never.' He managed a smile as he reached out to link his fingers with hers where her hand rested on their baby. 'I'll be rapt as long as both of you are happy and healthy.'

And he'd do a much better job of protecting his daughter than he'd managed with his sister.

CHAPTER TEN

Liz blinked at the rapidly blurring sight of Jack's fingers intertwined with hers. How stupid to ask if he was disappointed. The man didn't want to be a father—why would he care if they had a boy or a girl? Though most men had a gut reaction about wanting a son. Someone to carry on the family name.

Would Jack have been happier if she'd been carrying his son? Not that it'd made any difference with her own father—he'd ignored both her and her brother with cold impartiality.

Jack's answer was the very best she could hope for. He'd been more accepting of his position as a father-to-be than she'd expected. She shouldn't want more. And yet part of her wanted much, *much* more.

Jack's thumb began to rub slowly along her index finger. The tiny caress was mesmerising, almost unbearably sensual. She'd always loved his hands. So strong and intrinsically masculine. She sealed her lips against an avalanche of silly, need-filled questions that pushed to be spoken.

Did he still love her? He hadn't said it since he'd been back. He'd never been a man who spoke of his feelings often. And she hadn't found it necessary to hear it before. But now... Pregnancy stripped her emotions to a raw dependency, shaking her usual confidence. An unsolicited declaration of love would be a balm.

Did he want to hold her or was her rounded body repulsive to him? She longed for a hug, for some physical contact from him with a desperation that frightened her. How could she ask for his touch? Asking would diminish the gift.

'Liz?'

She turned her head slowly to find him watching her intently through brooding, half-closed eyes. Her heart turned over as his gaze slipped down to her mouth and lingered there. The urge to slide her tongue out to moisten her lips, to leave them parted provocatively, was overwhelming.

'Yes?' she managed, her voice rough. She swallowed, waited, hardly daring to breathe.

After a long, charged moment he leaned forward, his midnight-blue eyes still holding hers as he touched his lips to her mouth. So gentle, so undemanding that she could feel emotion welling in her chest again. His lips rubbed hers softly and her eyelids fluttered closed with the delicious sensations. She could feel his breath on her cheek and a faint rasp of his five-o'clock shadow. His teeth grazed her bottom lip lightly.

When he would have broken the contact, she leaned towards him, holding his mouth with hers. Would she have to beg for more of his kiss, for his touch? She sensed his hesitation. A reluctance. Fear and humiliation trickled into her stomach. Had she disgusted him with her hunger?

Just as she was about to pull away, his arm curved across her back, drawing her closer until her head was cradled on his shoulder. His other hand curled around her neck, tilting her chin, holding her as he deepened the kiss. His lips were firm and commanding on her mouth. She twisted towards him, running her hand across his nape, spearing her fingers into his hair.

He groaned softly, scooping her onto his lap, his arm resting on her belly as his hand splayed over her lower back. Her right breast was pressed to his chest and her body revelled in the contact as the kiss went on.

How had she ever thought she could live without this?

She murmured a protest as a frantic flurry of kicks erupted in her belly.

'Uh-oh.' Jack broke off the kiss slowly and rested his forehead on hers. She could hear his uneven breathing and delight blossomed in her chest. He wasn't immune to her. 'Someone's not impressed.'

His hand moved from her spine and began rubbing her stomach in soothing circles, spreading warmth across her tight skin.

Liz sighed. 'She's the only one, though.'

'Yeah. I've been wanting to do that since I got home,' he murmured. 'You're a mean kisser, Mrs Campbell.'

She swallowed hard. His words had her teetering on the verge of weeping again.

He chuckled. 'Our daughter has very bad timing.'

Her answering laugh was more of a small hiccup. But her urge to cry evaporated and she was grateful to him for dispelling the tension.

'Yes, she does, doesn't she?' She drew back and looked into his face.

His slow smile made her heart lurch.

A muffled beep sounded impatiently from her bag where it hung over the back of a dining chair. She sighed. 'I'd better get that.'

'You're not on call, are you?' he said as he helped her to her feet, his hands warm on her hips as he steadied her.

She straightened her clothing self-consciously, her skin hyper-sensitive to the movement of the fabric.

'No. I'm hoping it'll be the OB in Melbourne returning my call about Sarah.' Aware of Jack just a pace behind her, Liz walked across to the table and rummaged in her bag for the beeper. 'He wasn't available when I called earlier.'

'I'll get dinner started while you make the call.'

'Thanks.' She shivered as he brushed her hair aside to press a small kiss on the nape of her neck. It took a moment to focus her mind on the workings of the little device in her hands so she could retrieve the number she needed to ring.

Jack listened to the murmur of Liz's voice on the telephone. Felt the tension built by their embrace begin to ease out of his body. His wife was one very sexy woman. He had to remind himself she was nearly seven months pregnant and wouldn't be interested in fooling around.

Just as well she had her own on-board sentry to keep him in line. He grinned as he looked down at his arm, remembering the fluttery feeling of the baby's objection to having her mother manhandled.

The baby. His baby. A girl. He was going to be the father of a little girl. The magnitude of it hit him again. A daughter who was going to depend on him to make wise decisions, to provide guidance, a good example.

A peculiar uncertainty held him motionless at the sink for a long minute.

Had his mother felt this dilemma, this almost paralysing doubt about her ability to make the right decisions? Her usual approach to life had seemed to be to make no decision rather than take charge. But, thinking about it now, he realised that was a decision of sorts. He'd been filled with impotent rage after his sister had died. His mother had done nothing to care for the toddler that fateful day. Back then, he'd been certain he'd have done better.

And again at eighteen, when Kylie told him she was pregnant, he'd been so sure of his ability to handle things.

Now, sixteen years later, instead of feeling wiser and even more sure of himself he felt…terrified.

But he wasn't going to falter. Not when Liz and his daughter needed him. He was going to take charge and if his decisions weren't always right, at least he'd know he'd done the best he could.

He ran a hand around the base of his neck. *Oh, God.* One day his daughter was going to be a teenager—full of righteousness and confidence and attitude.

Knowing everything.

Knowing nothing.

Just like he had.

And the world was a different place now, so much faster, so many more reasons to be cautious. Today's pitfalls had potentially catastrophic consequences. Drugs, mobile phones that doubled as spy cameras, creeps on the Internet. And what would be around in another eighteen years when his daughter was ready to date?

She wasn't setting foot outside the house until he had to let her out to vote. He smiled wryly at his first decision—a knee-jerk, unrealistic pledge that didn't have a hope.

But somebody had to protect her from testosterone-ridden youths. Like he'd been. Lord, why on earth had Kylie's mother let *him* anywhere near her daughter?

Not that he'd done anything sleazy. Not like some of the males around these days with the party drugs that seemed to be a part of the kids' social scene. And date-rape drugs. What sort of pervert resorted to those measures to get laid?

If anyone did that to his daughter they'd have him to answer to.

Liz was home early again. The thought gave Jack a quiet sense of satisfaction as he pulled into the garage and parked beside her car. *Good.* She'd been more relaxed the last couple of days. Even resting until he got home without him having to nag. Since Sunday. Since their embrace, in fact. As though something had shifted mentally for her and she accepted that he was in this family for the long haul.

He ran a hand over his face, feeling the grit on his skin. He wrinkled his nose at the acrid smell embedded in the material of his overalls. Smoke and ash. House fire, the type he least enjoyed fighting. The elderly owner must have collected every newspaper since the *Dustin Courier* had started printing a century earlier and stored them in the hallway and near exits. The woman was now safely tucked into hospital suffering from mild smoke inhalation. She'd been lucky. They'd *all* been lucky. It could have ended very differently. None of the crew liked going to fires that involved a fatality.

Jack decided he'd have a shower and then wake Liz.

He crossed the patio, frowning when he realised the sliding security door was unlocked. In the dining room two large rubbish bags sat bulging on the floor and kitchen paraphernalia bristled from a box on the table. *What was going on?*

Muffled sounds came from down the hall. He walked through the house and realised that each room was getting the same treatment. Overflowing bags and boxes were scattered about on the floor.

For a weird, suspended moment he wondered if Liz had decided he had to go after all. He peered into one of the bags standing in the main bedroom door and was relieved to see some of her old clothes packed in there.

'Liz?'

'I'm in here. In the nursery.'

He strode down the hall to the room and stopped, stock still, in the doorway, his mouth hanging open.

'Bloody hell!'

She looked around and gave him a brief, tight smile before turning her attention back to the flippers and goggles in her hands. 'Thank goodness you're here. Look, do you think you're going to want this diving gear again? If you do, it's really going to have to go out in the shed.'

'What are you doing?'

'Organising things for when the baby arrives.' She tossed the gear into an open box at her feet and looked back into the wardrobe.

'Does it have to be done tonight?'

'Yes.' She sounded determined, hearty, but he noticed her hand was shaking when she lifted it to her brow. 'We haven't done anything. Nothing at all. Our little girl hasn't got anywhere to live, has she?'

'Liz…'

He watched her reach into the cupboard to tug on the straps of a leather bag. He recognised his ten-pin bowling ball carrier. He stepped forward and took it out of her hands. 'Stop it, sweetheart. You shouldn't be lifting all this stuff in your condition. What's got into you?'

'Someone has to do something. *I* have to do something. I got a lovely carry-cot for the baby from the nurses at the hospital today and the nursery's a mess. Look at it.' Her voice rose a notch and wobbled slightly as she waved her hand around in an expansive arc. 'It's just a giant junk room.'

'Yes, but why does it have to be done right this minute, darlin'?' he said, using his most soothing tones. 'Can't it wait until we've had dinner? At least until I've had a shower?'

She focussed on him properly then and he saw her expression change to horror. 'Oh, God. Look at you. You're filthy, Jack. Get out of the nursery. Get out.' She made shooing motions with her hands. 'You're probably dropping all sorts of horrid dust and debris and you smell like an old fireplace.'

He sighed and retreated to the door. 'I'll have a quick shower. In the meantime, try not to throw out *all* my old stuff, will you?'

She smiled weakly.

'Why don't you sit down until I come back?' He sighed when she gave him the expected negative response. 'Just promise me you won't lift anything heavy, okay? I haven't been to any of those prenatal classes yet so I don't know what to do if you decide to give birth right here on the floor.' He'd meant the words to lighten the moment, but the look she sent him was stark with horror. 'Hey, I'm joking, darling.'

In the bathroom, he stripped off his overalls and turned on the water. *What had changed? Something must have for Liz's behaviour to have done such an about-face.* They'd made great strides, but now everything seemed to have gone sour. He stepped under the stream of water, racking his brain to no avail for something he might have done to upset her. This morning they'd had a very friendly breakfast together before going their separate ways.

He soaped himself quickly, his mind on the expression on her face. Liz was afraid. His heart stumbled. Was there something wrong with her? She didn't look ill. She looked gorgeous, radiant and…worried.

He finished his shower in record time and dragged on a pair of comfortable old jeans and a T-shirt.

Back at the nursery, he found Liz staring into a half-filled box on the rocking chair, her arms wrapped tightly around her body.

'Liz?'

She started at the sound of his voice, her hands jerking into action as though someone was pulling an invisible string. She grabbed something out of the box and held it up. One of his old shirts. 'What about this? I don't think I've ever seen you wearing it.'

'Stop for a minute.' He reached for her, turning her so he could tug the shirt from her grasp. He tossed it back in the box and held her hands until her reluctant gaze came up to meet his. 'Speak to me, sweetheart. What's the urgency here? What's changed since this morning?'

Tears welled in her eyes and spilled onto her cheeks. She seemed to wilt before his eyes. 'It's the baby.'

Dread clutched his stomach with cold fingers.

'What about the baby? Is there something wrong with her?'

'No, she's. Fine. But she's…c-coming four w-weeks earlier.' She spoke haltingly, the words struggling out, almost incoherent around huge sobs.

Jack swore softly and scooped her up into his arms, feeling the quiver running through her slight frame. Her arms came up to cling to him and she pressed her face into his neck. He hugged her to him for a moment then looked around for somewhere to sit. The clearest surface was an old blanket chest beneath the window so he carefully picked a course to that and settled her on his lap.

He held her while she cried, rocking slightly, waiting until the worst was over. 'Any gentleman worth his salt would offer you a snowy white handkerchief about now.' He shifted slightly, groping under his thigh and pulling out the lump that he'd been half sitting on. A peanut-shaped cushion. 'I don't suppose this will do?'

He was rewarded with a watery chuckle. 'Thanks, but I've got my own.' She blew her nose then settled back against his shoulder.

He laid his cheek against the top of her head and waited for her to speak.

'Tony sent me for another scan and it confirmed that I was a month out.' Her voice was low and steady.

'Oh.' He took in the words, turned them over. 'But wouldn't you know? I mean, what about…? Doesn't your period stop when you're pregnant?'

'Usually, yes. And the due date is calculated by using the date of the last menstruation.' She sighed. 'But Tony thinks that I must have been pregnant even though I was still bleeding. He did query my dates after the first scan, but I didn't really think it was possible.'

'I see. Bit of a shock, huh?'

He felt her nod, her hair brushing under his chin.

'But the baby's okay, isn't she?'

'Yes.' Her agitated fingers pleated and twisted one corner of the handkerchief.

'Okay, then. We can deal with this.' He did some mental calculations. 'The baby's still not due for…what? Six weeks?'

She nodded again.

'Right. So this weekend, we can go shopping on Saturday morning. Splurge on all the things we need for her. You make the list.' He looked around the room. 'It doesn't need painting in here. And I can organise the gear. Easy, darlin'. The job's as good as done. We just have to wait for her ladyship to make her appearance.'

He felt her begin to shake, listened as another huge sob escaped.

'Hey? What did I say wrong?'

'Nothing.' She sniffled and squeezed out words in small bursts. 'You're. Being. So good about this.'

'And that's why you're crying?' He stroked her back in circles, hoping to soothe her.

'It's not that.' She gulped and blew her nose again. 'It's me. I'm ruining everything.'

'Tell me how you're ruining everything?'

'You don't want children and I've trapped you into staying because I'm pregnant. And I don't know how to make it work.' Her words tumbled out, running into each other in her hurry to get them said. 'And I'm going to be a terrible mother.'

'You're going to be a fabulous mother,' he said, latching onto the last thing she'd said while he tried to sort out the others.

'And we haven't got a name for her. We haven't even discussed it.'

'Emma.' The name popped out, catching him by surprise. Had his subconscious been working on the idea since he'd found out their baby was going to be a girl? Now he'd said it aloud, there was a sense of rightness about it.

'Emma?'

'Hmm.' He touched her stomach, stroked the taut fabric, feeling the hard warmth of the baby mound. 'If you like it.' This was the perfect opportunity to broach the subject of the toddler's death, but the words felt as though they needed to be wrenched from some deep emotional well. 'My sister's name.'

'You have a sister? You never told me.'

'Had.' His hand stilled and he meet her gaze. 'She died when I was thirteen. Meningitis.'

'Oh, Jack.' Her green-gold eyes were filled with tenderness. 'How awful.'

'Yeah.' He reached up to wipe the residue of teardrops from her cheeks with his thumb. 'I felt responsible for a long time.'

'But how could you? You were a child, too.'

'I was thirteen. I knew Em was sick. She was vomiting and cranky when I tried to pick her up to comfort her. I could feel how feverish she was.' He sighed. 'And I left her with Janet.'

'But you were a child yourself, darling. What choice did you have?' He could hear her anger on his behalf.

'I made Janet promise to take her to the hospital or I wouldn't go to school. She promised because the school had been on her back about my truancy.' He shrugged. 'Maybe she meant it when she made the promise, but after I left she must have got into her stash instead.'

Liz's arm came around his shoulder and she held him. Her support gave him the encouragement he needed to tell her the rest of it.

'I went home at lunchtime and found them both unconscious. Em was covered in spots. The ambulance came and took them both to hospital. Janet lived. Em died later that day.' His mouth twisted, the taste of bitter grief as fresh as though it were yesterday. 'And I wished it had been the other way around.'

'Oh, darling. You must have been so angry.'

'Yeah. And I made sure Janet knew how much. Not long after that she overdosed.'

'You still feel guilty for what happened to them, don't you?' Tears welled in her eyes and he knew they were for him.

'Don't, sweetheart.'

'Why not? Someone should weep for you and Emma. You were a little boy carrying an adult's responsibility. And it wasn't fair.' She leaned forward and wrapped her arms around him. Her pregnant stomach pressed against him quietly as though even the baby appreciated the gravity of the moment. 'It was Janet's job to look after both of you. Not yours to look after everyone.'

He held her as tightly as she held him. And after a while he realised his pain wasn't quite as sharp, wasn't quite as poisonous.

CHAPTER ELEVEN

EMMA CAMPBELL.

The name had a nice ring to it.

Liz found her thoughts on Jack's revelations again after Tony relieved her for a late break the next morning. She decided to go across to the cafeteria for a cappuccino.

'Nasty wind today,' said the woman behind the counter as she heated the milk for the coffee.

'Yes. Days like this are a real worry.' Liz glanced out the window where the smaller branches of the gnarled old oak were dipping and waving in a wild dance. 'Hopefully the cool change will arrive earlier and give us a good soaking.'

'Yes. I heard there's already been a couple of callouts for spot fires. People using tractors in long grass. Never seem to learn that a hot exhaust will start a fire quick as look at you.'

'Thanks,' said Liz, accepting the aromatic frothy drink. 'I suppose Bill's on call, is he?'

'Yes. He's glad your Jack took the captain's job. All the boys are.' The woman rang up the till then turned to Liz with a grin. 'Though not as pleased as you are to see him back, I suppose. How long to go now?'

Liz rested her free hand on her stomach. 'Six weeks.'

'That soon. It seems to have passed so quickly.'

'That's easy for you to say.' Liz grinned, opting not to go into the details of her much closer due date.

The woman laughed. 'True. How are you coping with the heat?'

'Not too bad. I'm a bit tired.'

'Of course you are, dear, and here's me keeping you standing and talking. Off you go and take the chance to put your feet up while you can now.'

'I'll do that. Thanks.'

Not tempted to take advantage of the chairs outside because of the weather, Liz sat by the window, watching the trees as they bent and swayed with powerful wind gusts. She hoped the fire season wasn't going to be bad this year. Jack was good at his job, but it still worried her when he was out fighting fires on the total fire ban days like today. Even the most experienced firemen got it wrong sometimes.

While he'd been in the US, she'd felt isolated somehow from the daily risks he took. He'd been so far away and so out of touch that it'd all seemed faintly unreal. And she'd been struggling to come to terms with the discovery that she was pregnant.

But now he was back and he was talking to her more than he ever had before. He'd been amazing. So much more understanding than she would ever have expected her macho husband to be. While she still yearned for a declaration of love, she did have to applaud him for the sensitivity with which he'd handled her tears last night.

Her heart skipped when she replayed the words of reassurance he'd spoken as she'd got up to go to bed last night. *Liz, I'm not trapped in this marriage. I want to be here.* That was almost as good as an *I love you.* Almost.

Poor Jack.

She would never have guessed the things he'd been through, the things that had shaped the man he'd become. He didn't want her pity, but her heart went out to him, for the child he'd been, for what he'd suffered. His struggle to look after his little sister, and probably his mother as well, was typical of a child in his situation. He'd had responsibilities far beyond his tender years loaded onto his shoulders. Drug addicts and alcoholics were usually selfish parents.

She blew the foam away from the edge of her mug and took a sip.

No wonder he didn't want children of his own. He'd done his nurturing so young, under dreadful conditions and with such a tragic outcome. Jack had obviously loved little Emma deeply, been happy to be her knight in shining armour all those years ago. He'd been the one the toddler had turned to when she'd needed something. Losing her that way had left a burden of guilt that couldn't be lifted by a few sympathetic words. No matter how well chosen or well meant they were.

She needed to be practical about supporting him. Let go of her expectation for him to be an involved father. Help him succeed with whatever connection he was prepared to make with their daughter. Make sure having a child didn't become a burden for him, something to bring back awful memories from his childhood.

She'd been prepared to be a single parent anyway so doing the lion's share of the parenting wouldn't be a big deal. Any help he could give her would be a bonus. If he continued to do most of the cooking she would be content with that.

She expected to feel good for making such a commendable resolution. And she did. But at the same time she felt faintly uncomfortable—as though her altruism was somehow flawed.

And more doubts crowded in as she remembered her own advice to new mothers exhausted and suffering from sleep deprivation. She always gently chided them to ask for the help they needed from their partners, pointing out that the midwife ran an excellent set of pre- and post-natal classes. Looking back on her superior attitude made her wince slightly. How easy to say what someone else should do. How much better she appreciated the difficulties now that it looked like she might be in the same situation.

But she was used to working effectively despite lack of sleep. Being a new mother shouldn't be any worse, should it?

She arched her spine and rubbed the muscles of her lower back absent-mindedly. Being on her feet in the clinic was making her particularly tender today. Perhaps she should do a mid-stream urine and make sure she wasn't incubating a urinary tract infection. Not something she wanted to leave untreated at this late stage.

Lord, six weeks to go and she'd be a mother. She felt much more relaxed about the news today. And she knew that was largely due to Jack's reaction last night. He'd been marvellous. No wonder she loved him.

They had the prenatal class tonight. Her eyes moved to the window again. If the change didn't arrive with rain, Jack wouldn't be able to come. She didn't know if she felt glad or sorry.

The air in the car was thick with tension.

Jack glanced at Liz's profile. Her eyes were fixed on the road ahead as though a great truth would be revealed there and if she blinked she'd miss it. Her forehead was furrowed in a ferocious frown and the full, cushiony pout of her bottom lip was drawn in. She was obviously gnawing at the tender flesh.

He wondered what was going through her mind. Was it something that had happened at work today? Or was it tonight's class that was bothering her? She'd said again and again that she'd understand if he couldn't come. Almost as though she'd been hoping he'd have to work.

'Hey, I fed you before we left home,' he teased.

Her head jerked around and her eyes met his.

'What?' Her liberated lip was glossy with moisture. He

nearly groaned. Perhaps he should have just left her to devour it. Or he could offer to help her. He'd like that. Although he wondered how many more of those incendiary kisses his system could cope with.

'I thought you must still be hungry the way you're hoeing into your bottom lip.'

'Oh.' Her tongue came out, ran across the ruby surface and disappeared. 'I was just thinking about…the class.'

'Yeah, I kind of guessed that. Will it help if I promise to behave myself?'

Her eyebrows arched expressively. 'It's a class full of heavily pregnant women, Jack. What did you think you might get up to?'

He grinned and reached out to squeeze her hands lying clenched together on her lap. 'When you put it like that, gorgeous, not much.'

After a second her hands relaxed in his, one turning to link fingers. The intimate action filled him with contentment.

'Speaking of pregnant women, I went in to see Danny and Sarah in hospital yesterday. You've put her on bed rest as well. Some problem with her pregnancy.' He glanced at her to see her lips pursed.

'Hmm.'

'How is she?'

Her fingers twisted slightly in his clasp. He knew she wouldn't discuss Sarah's case specifically and he didn't expect her to, but he wanted to know a bit more about the condition.

'Didn't they tell you?'

'Sarah said something about clamps.'

'Pre-eclampsia.'

'What is it? Is it dangerous?'

'Potentially. But as long as it's caught early, the pregnancy can be monitored.' She answered his last question first and was silent for so long that for a moment or two he wondered if she was going to continue. 'Pre-eclampsia's a complicated condition that can cause high blood pressure and kidney problems, among other things. It can be bad for the mother as well as the baby if it's not treated. But usually it's picked up at the prenatal check-ups.'

'Sarah told me you had her baby wired for sound and that he's doing well.'

'Yes, he is.'

He could hear the relief in her voice and sympathised with her. Treating friends must be difficult.

'How common is it?'

'About ten per cent of pregnant women will get some degree of pre-eclampsia. Perhaps a bit less.'

'One in ten. That still seems high. What about someone like you?' he asked, getting to the issue that was really bothering him. 'You have a high-pressure job, does that put you at greater risk?'

He could feel her eyes on him, but he concentrated on the road.

'No.'

'So you won't get it?'

'I can't say that for sure, but there's no reason why I should.' Her fingers flexed around his, but she didn't release her hold.

'But you get checked regularly to make sure?' He couldn't stop himself from pressing.

'Yes. As you know, I saw Tony yesterday. There was no problem with my blood pressure,' she said dryly. 'It was my dates that were the big problem.'

'Yeah.' He turned his head and caught her wry look. 'But as problems go it's not so bad. You're not worried about that now, are you?'

She shrugged. 'There just seems so much to do.'

'And we'll get it all done.' He squeezed her hand lightly. 'Trust me.'

He was pleased when that elicited a small, reluctant chuckle from Liz.

'I know.' He grinned. 'Never trust a man who says *trust me*.'

There was a small, companionable silence.

'Danny's moaning about having to give up smoking or risk another lung collapse.'

'Hmm.'

'Mind you, he's a considerate moaner. He's only doing it while he's not in the room with Sarah.'

Liz chuckled. 'Yes. Poor Danny. Better for him if he can stop. It won't be easy, though.'

'No. I'm glad he's in hospital instead of at work. He's trying so hard to be cheerful and even-tempered for her sake, it's a wonder he hasn't ruptured something.'

He released her hand so he could make the turn into the car park. Out of the corner of his eye he saw her hands clench together again. At least he'd managed to take her mind off the class for a few minutes. Her tension was starting to get to him.

Surely the hands-on part that Liz had talked about couldn't be all that bad. Besides, he was looking forward to getting his hands on more of his wife. He'd enjoyed their kisses and cuddles over the last few days while he'd been comforting her. And she hadn't objected either. He just had to hold on to that thought for…another three months? Four? Suddenly his joking about Danny abstaining from cigarettes didn't seem so funny.

Served himself right.

Liz smiled weakly at the other couples who greeted them as she entered the classroom with Jack. Most of them were already slouched back in the beanbags, the women sitting between their partners thighs, their backs supported on their partners' chests. They looked so comfortable…so cosy… Oh, God. So much more intimate than they had in the previous sessions.

'Pull up a beanbag,' said one of the pregnant women. 'Julie just had to duck out and grab the video.'

Liz's pulse jumped wildly at the thought of sitting with Jack holding her that way. She didn't dare meet his eyes lest he read her nervousness.

'Okay, guys. It looks like everyone's here.' Julie, the young midwife, breezed into the class, followed by a couple of orderlies pushing the television and video trolley. While they manoeuvred it into position at the front of the class, she said, 'I hope we've all been doing our exercises.'

'Have we?' Jack murmured in her ear as his hand caught hers and tugged her over to a spare beanbag.

'Yes.' Her voice came out as a croak.

'Aren't we good?'

She watched him plump the bag and sit down, his long legs spreading to form a niche for her. He held his hand out to her, a challenging look on his face. 'Come on, darlin'. You're making the place look untidy.'

She swallowed and sank awkwardly into position. Her breath came in short gasps as she tried to cope with having her body enveloped by his. She could feel his hard thighs alongside her hips, the warmth of him at her back, his breath on her neck. Her light clothes were no barrier against feeling his chest expand with each breath he took.

She closed her eyes, but that made the sensations even more dramatic.

'Hmm. I could get to like this. We're getting a beanbag.' The rumble of his voice sent an internal shiver through her.

Relaxing music filled the classroom. 'You can all do your Kegels while I organise the video player. Partners can do them, too. No reason why you should lounge in comfort.'

'What on earth is a Kegel?' Jack growled in her ear.

'Pelvic-floor exercise,' she said shortly.

'These are great for helping with the delivery, and for your recovery afterwards,' Julie said from the front. 'And the added benefit is they're great for your sex life.'

Liz felt a rush of need swamp her, settling as an ache low in her abdomen. The last thing she needed to think about was sex. Not while she was snugly surrounded by her husband. Not when they hadn't made love for so, *so* long. *Oh, God. What was Jack thinking?*

'Bonus,' quipped one of the other fathers-to-be.

'Amen,' murmured Jack.

'Anyone had any problems? No? Excellent. Okay, tonight I want to talk about pain relief. Then we'll do our stretches and have a nice relaxation before watching the birth video.'

Relaxation? In this position? Liz suppressed the giggle that threatened to escape, half-afraid it would descend out of control into hysterical laughter.

With Jack so close to her, Liz could feel his intense focus on Julie's talk about analgesia during delivery. She frowned as she remembered his suggestion about having a Caesarean. He'd dropped the issue after she'd reassured him but she'd been left with the nagging conviction that he hadn't been happy.

'Any questions?' Julie wrapped up the segment and moved on. 'Okay, since we've all got partners tonight I want to do some extended stretches.'

Liz worked carefully through the positions, keeping her concentration on her movements, trying to dampen her response to Jack's touch. She thought she was doing well until Julie had them pretzelled into a twist.

'Ladies, I want you to breathe into the stretch and relax.'

Just about impossible with Jack leaning over her, his warm hands on her knee and her thigh. The pressure of his fingers branded her gently.

'Partners, you can help relax her by rubbing these points.' Julie was obviously demonstrating the position because a moment later Jack's hand smoothed up her thigh and across her buttock.

She almost whimpered with pleasure. His touch was wonderful. *His touch was torture.* She was consumed with the thought of him making love to her. Could she ask him to? Could she be that bold? But what if he thought her pregnant body was unattractive? He'd been so fantastic she didn't want to upset the link they'd forged since he'd come home. She bit down on a sob of frustration.

She couldn't ask.

'Are you all right? Am I pressing too hard?'

'No, no. S-something in my eye.'

'Vary the pressure,' instructed Julie. 'Partners, massage is a tool for you to take into the birthing room. Practise it as often as you can. But don't forget that when it comes to the actual delivery there might be times when she doesn't want to be touched so try to tune into what she needs.'

Jack's hands had touched her nearly everywhere. Rubbing her lower back while she knelt on her hands and knees, kneading her shoulders while she practised squatting, stroking her stomach while she was relaxing. She'd watched his face then, seen the smile that played around his mouth as the baby pushed back against his pressure. He looked…enthralled. Not at all like a man who didn't want children. Could he be changing his mind? She looked away, blinking back the sudden urge to weep for him.

By the time Julie was ready to put on the video, every inch of Liz's skin felt as though it had been caressed and kneaded. Exhausted from the roller-coaster of physical and emotional sensations that had racketed through her during the evening, she settled back in the beanbag with Jack.

His arms came around her, holding her, his hands on hers and his cheek beside her hair. The position was undeniably comfortable and just sitting, resting against his body as they waited for the programme to start, was bliss.

The video was a shock.

Sure, she'd delivered babies, knew all the technicalities, the correct terms, the potential problems and interventions that might be necessary for a birth. Perhaps if her path to getting pregnant had been smooth and planned, the idea of Jack being at the birth would have been a delight. Instead, the images flashing on the screen drove home the confronting intimacy of the experience they would share in six weeks.

With her mind in turmoil, she didn't notice Jack's tension until the video reached the delivery scene. His fingers tightened on hers as the woman moaned in pain. The minor discomfort made her aware of the stiffness in his frame surrounding her. She looked up to see his face carved in grim lines.

'Jack?'

'Hmm?' A muscle in his jaw jumped, but he didn't take his eyes off the screen.

Liz turned back to watch the rest of the straightforward delivery. She sighed in resignation. His push for a Caesarean was probably going to take on a whole new impetus after this.

Liz searched for the words to reassure him as he slid into the driver's seat a little later. She looked at his profile, the set jaw, the tight mouth. His hands on the steering-wheel flexed as he sat staring moodily through the windscreen.

'It won't seem so graphic when you're in the birthing suite, Jack.'

'Why?' He turned, focussing his brooding gaze on her. 'Will you have a Caesarean?'

'No. But—'

'Or an epidural?'

'Not if I don't need one, no.'

'Then I don't see how you can give me that reassurance.'

Liz regarded him somberly for a moment. 'What is it that's worrying you about this?'

'I was a big baby. My sister was a big baby.' He grimaced.

'We nearly ripped Janet apart when she gave birth to us. She was lucky to survive.'

'Did she tell you that?'

'Yes. Often.'

Was there no end to the guilt his mother had been prepared to burden him with? Liz looked down at her hands clasped in her lap. How was she going to fight the damage done to the man she loved?

'Jack, your—Janet had an illness. Her drug addiction made her say things that no one should say to a child. You have to let those things go.' She wasn't reaching him at all. She touched his arm, feeling the tautness of his muscles. 'Darling, you don't have to come to the birth if you don't want to.'

He shifted, reaching for the ignition, breaking the contact. Liz squeezed her eyes shut, trying not to let his action hurt. He'd come so far, she had to give him time. But their baby was due in six short weeks. So little time to heal all the scars his mother had left.

'I'll be there.'

CHAPTER TWELVE

LIZ wandered into the nursery, pausing for a moment in the doorway to enjoy the cheery feel of the room. Hard to believe this time last week it had been a glorified storage room. Everything was ready for little Emma's arrival thanks to Jack's mammoth effort on the weekend.

Everything was ready...*except Emma's father.*

He'd withdrawn in some way that Liz found hard to define. She trailed her hand over the soft, embroidered blanket folded at the end of the cot. He wasn't rude or difficult. He didn't spend hours at the fire station. He looked after her, cooking meals and insisting she rest whenever possible.

But on odd occasions over the last week she'd caught him staring at her belly as though it was a problem that he needed to solve.

His unhappiness was palpable. She longed to reach out to him and had done so several times, hoping to soothe the tension that radiated from him. He tolerated her touch, but seemed relieved when she retreated.

Talking wasn't working either. He simply wouldn't discuss it and she was at a loss to know quite how to tackle the issue. Butting up against his strong, silent façade made her realise how much things had changed over the weeks since he'd returned. And she enjoyed those changes even while some small corner of her still struggled with her inexplicable ambivalence.

He was doing all the things he'd promised and more. She looked around the room, appreciating the butter-yellow walls and jolly cartoon figures cavorting across two surfaces. They'd spent hours shopping on Saturday, with Jack gently but firmly making sure she took breaks while he trundled gear out to the car.

Then, on Sunday, he'd sat her in the rocking chair to direct proceedings. Not that he'd really needed her there while he'd assembled furniture, hung the pictures, mobiles and curtains. Drawers had been packed exactly as she'd requested with the clothes and nappies and all the paraphernalia required by a newborn.

He'd made up the bassinette bedding, his large, tanned hands incongruous against the fluffy weave of the small blankets. Watching him work with such care had made her want to cry. Again.

She picked up a rainbow-coloured teddy that was sitting on the corner of the dresser, her fingers sinking into the plump, soft body. Its goofy grin drew a tremulous smile from her.

She longed to be able to find the words to help Jack through this patch, but each time she tried to broach the subject of the delivery he shut her out. She tried to explain that the labour process could be beneficial to mother and baby if it was allowed to progress naturally.

Her body was designed to give birth, she'd told him earnestly, and was preparing itself to do just that.

A tiny, watery chuckle escaped as she remembered the look of horror her comment had elicited. So much for the comfort she'd been hoping to give him. Had he wondered if she might give birth right then and there?

Even promising that she'd let Julie and Tony guide her at the birth if they thought painkillers or a Caesarean were absolutely necessary hadn't eased his mind.

She wished she could get hold of the old maternity hospital notes for his mother. But the institution had closed and no one seemed to be able to tell her where the records were stored or if they'd been destroyed. Liz sighed, wondering if she'd done the right thing by deciding not to tell Jack about her enquiries. It seemed pointless since she couldn't tell him the facts about his birth. Had it been the horror story Janet had related to her son or had she embellished it for dramatic value? Just the way he'd phrased it, words repeated from his past, smacked of histrionics.

She propped the teddy back on the dresser.

Blast the woman for using such an ill-chosen weapon to frighten an impressionable thirteen-year-old.

'Everything all right?'

Liz turned at the sound of Jack's voice. He was lounging in the doorway, arms folded with his shoulder against the jamb. She wondered if he'd been standing there long. 'Yes, fine.'

'Ready to go?'

The prenatal class. Liz sighed. What topics would they be covering tonight? Something else that might drive the wedge more firmly between them? If only she'd discouraged him from coming last week.

She managed a smile. 'Yes, thanks.'

Fortunately, the class went much more smoothly, with Julie covering the stages of labour. It seemed as though the midwife had thrown all the curly issues into last week's session and today she wanted to steer clear of confronting topics.

Even so, Jack's attention was absolute. If Liz hadn't understood the reasons behind his concentration, she might have been tempted to tease him that he'd be able to deliver their daughter himself.

He helped her through the stretches. Her body hummed with vitality as it soaked up his touch. His massage during the relaxation session was particularly exquisite torture.

To take her mind off his hands stroking her stomach, she studied him.

His face, with its strong, angular planes and lean cheeks was so dear to her. He was a good-looking man. Not in a flashy, pin-up way, but with a quiet, somehow reassuring masculinity. There was just a sprinkling of grey hair at his temple. He'd age well, look distinguished in another ten to twenty years. She smiled slightly as she acknowledged that he already looked distinguished.

Her eyes moved onto his mouth and traced the firm, well-shaped lips. The grooves in his cheeks that creased mischievously when he smiled were nearly invisible while his face was composed with concentration.

His eyes were downcast as he worked over every inch of her pregnant belly so she couldn't see their piercing blue. The way his black lashes drooped slightly at the outer corners of his eyes gave him an air of sleepy sensuality. Deceptive because she knew there was nothing remotely slumberous about him, particularly not when he was bent on making love to her.

Oh, God. She *mustn't* let her mind wander along that track, not while he was touching her. Hoping to ward off the sudden attack of breathlessness that threatened, she took a deep lungful of air.

His hands stilled on her as his eyes, sharp and questioning, sought hers. 'Liz?'

She felt a small thrill of panic. He always saw too much.

'Sorry. Just a bit of, um, reflux.' She forced a smile, hoping he wouldn't see through her quick fabrication. She didn't want to even hint at her capricious thoughts with the way things stood between them. What would he think of her?

'Oh, God.' His blue eyes widened suddenly with astonishment before he let out a short laugh. 'That was both feet. I think you've got the Karate Kid in there.'

Glad to be distracted from her thoughts, she relaxed and grinned up at him. 'It feels like that sometimes.'

He looked back down at her stomach. 'Do you think I can get her to do it again?'

'You can try. You never know.' And if it kept his hands on her, Liz realised, she wouldn't be sorry. She was a sad case. Fairness made her add, 'But I think your daughter has developed great timing for the last word so don't be disappointed if she doesn't co-operate.'

Later that evening, after a relaxing bath, Liz smoothed cream over the tight skin of her belly. Her lips curved as she replayed the magical moment she'd shared with Jack in the class. His delight in his daughter's silent communication had been wonderful to witness. And even though the baby hadn't been enticed to give a repeat performance, he hadn't minded.

Good for you, Emma. If I can't help your daddy, perhaps you can. Now, if we could just make him comfortable with your method of arrival, things would be—

'Liz, have you seen—?'

She gasped and swung to face the door. Jack was standing in the middle of the bedroom, his mouth open, his gaze riveted on her nearly naked form. In a microsecond his air of irritated abstraction was gone.

Her hands automatically moved to cover herself while a small corner of her mind acknowledged it was a futile exercise. She watched his eyes slowly track down her body. When he raised them again to her face she saw the bright blue had darkened to something sensual and possessive.

He swallowed. Even with her eyes fixed on his she could see the convulsive slide of his throat. She felt herself swallow in unison.

'You don't need to cover yourself, Liz.' His voice was low and husky. 'You're beautiful.'

'I'm pregnant.' She sounded desperately breathless.

'Mmm.' His gaze made the trek to her belly and back to her eyes. She couldn't doubt the sincerity she saw there. 'Pregnant *and* beautiful.'

He moved towards her, slowly, almost cautiously. As though he expected her to bolt. Didn't he realise she was frozen to the spot? Her body quivered with each hard, pounding beat of her heart. Unable to endure the intensity of his stare, she slid her focus down, fixing it on the rapid pulse that throbbed in his throat. She moistened her lips as he came to a halt in front of her.

The suspense was unbearable. Why didn't he touch her, put her out of her misery? She was almost ready to beg when his hands lifted to her shoulders. A sigh of pleasure escaped as his long, strong fingers curled around her upper arms, sliding slowly down. The backs of his thumbs brushed the sides of her full, aching breasts lightly, so lightly the touch was indescribably exciting.

Because he was taller than she was, he easily bent over the baby bump. His head angled into the crook of her neck, his lips nuzzling her nape before he grazed his teeth over the sensitive flesh. Her response exploded through her body, leaving her weak and shaky.

He moved to her side as his hand stroked her naked stomach. His palms were slightly rough, rasping her taut skin as he made small circles. She lifted her face, sliding her hand into his thick, dark hair to bring his mouth down to hers. The kiss was delicious, a teasing caress full of promise.

'I need you, Liz.' He tightened his arm around her shoulders, cuddling her even closer to his body.

'Yes.'

'Please.' His lips trailed small kisses over her face. 'Let me make love to you.'

Oh, yes, that was she wanted, too. *So much.* But they had to be careful. They had more than just themselves to consider, now. The baby. She had to think of the baby's safety. She could hardly process the words to get them out, her body was one big shiver of sensation.

'Have you got any protection?' she gasped as he nibbled his way down the muscle of her throat and traced her clavicle with the tip of his tongue.

'Why, sweetheart? You won't get any more pregnant.'

She could feel the warm huff of his breath on her skin as he chuckled.

'No…no, I meant…is it safe? F-for the baby? H-have you been with anyone else? While you were away?' She pushed the questions out with an enormous effort.

Jack froze before his head jerked back as if she'd hit him.

'Hell, Liz.' His shocked eyes bored into hers and she could see his nostrils flare with a sharply inhaled breath. 'What sort of question is that? If you don't want me to touch you, all you have to do is say no.'

He stepped away and her body chilled instantly with the loss of his warmth. She stood mute, wanting to curl away from his disgust.

Wishing she could take the words back.

Needing an answer. Her heart felt as though it would shatter.

He spun on his heel and strode out of the room, shutting the door with a tiny, controlled snick. The sound snapped her out of her daze.

Pushing back tears, she thrust her arms into her shirt and struggled to fasten the buttons with trembling fingers.

How dare he hide behind injured male pride over this? She dragged on a pair of capri pants, fighting to get her feet through the clinging fabric. All she'd done was ask a perfectly reasonable question. Her timing might not have been ideal, but she was still entitled to an answer.

She flung open the door and stalked down to the kitchen.

The door out to the patio was open. She stepped through and saw him at the railing, his hands braced as he stared moodily out into the night.

'Well?'

He didn't bother to turn. 'Well, what?'

'You haven't answered my question, Jack.'

'What does your female intuition tell you, Liz?'

'I want to hear it from you.' She leaned against the rail a couple of metres away from him, examining his grim profile, knowing the distance between them had never been greater.

'You think I've been unfaithful.' His voice was flat, full of hurt.

'That's not fair. I think I have a right to know. For my sake and for our baby's sake.'

'Yeah, I guess you do.' He sighed, a sad, defeated sound that made her heart quail. 'But I'd like to think you trust me.'

'Like you trust me?' She wrapped her arms tightly around her body. She wanted to be sensible about this. They'd parted on the brink of divorce. In theory, he'd have been free to play around. But she knew in her heart it would feel like betrayal. 'You can ask me if the baby's yours, but I can't ask if you've slept with someone while you were away?'

'I've wondered why you haven't asked me about that.' A muscle rippled in his jaw before he straightened and turned to look at her, his eyes shadowed but steady. 'I haven't slept with anyone else. I wanted to… I'm not proud of the fact that I was going to. But I didn't.'

'You—you didn't?' The words seemed hard to comprehend.

'No.' Unequivocal.

She felt herself sag in relief, was tempted to leave it at that. But she needed to know it all now. 'But—but we'd agreed to a divorce before you went, so why didn't you feel free to do what you wanted?'

He laughed, but the sound was hollow, unamused. 'Oh, I

tried to feel free, Liz. But it didn't work.' He shrugged. 'Something stopped me. It felt…like I was being unfaithful.'

'Oh.'

'Yeah, oh.' He gave her a wry smile. 'I couldn't put someone else…couldn't put *you* through that pain.'

'Someone else?' Thoughts tumbled through her mind. Had Jack been unfaithful in a previous relationship? *No*, if he was too principled to sleep with another woman when his marriage seemed doomed then he wouldn't have done that. Enlightenment struck. 'Someone's been unfaithful to you, haven't they?'

He nodded. 'Come and sit down inside, Liz. There are some things you should know.'

She didn't resist, couldn't resist, as he led her back inside. He pushed her gently down onto the sofa and, keeping hold of her hand, sat beside her.

'When I was eighteen…' He stopped and Liz looked up to find him watching her.

When he didn't go on, she said softly, 'Tell me, darling. Help me understand. Please.'

He sighed. 'It's not a very edifying tale. When I was eighteen, my girlfriend fell pregnant. We got engaged. I wanted to do the right thing.'

His thumb rubbed over her wedding ring as they sat in silence for a long moment. 'Kylie lost the baby.' His voice sounded almost dreamy, as though he was looking back down the years to see those distant events. 'I was…devastated. I'm not really sure why it affected me so much. Kylie was relieved. Maybe I should have been, too. Or maybe I thought I could make up for failing Emma.'

'*You* didn't fail Emma, Jack. Your mother did.' She squeezed his hand.

He made a noncommittal sound. 'I wanted us to get married regardless of losing the baby. Kylie saw a chance to shake off her small-town roots. And a chance to shake off her small-town boyfriend. Unfortunately, I was a bit dim so she told me she didn't know if I was her baby's father. I suppose she thought quick cruelty would save a lingering break-up.'

'You must have been terribly hurt.' The women in his young life had treated him abominably. No wonder his gut reaction had been to think her baby was someone else's. It still hurt, but at least now she understood.

'Mmm. And angry. I made some rash vows to myself about how I'd behave in future relationships.' He lifted her hand to his mouth and kissed the sensitive skin at her wrist. 'I didn't break any of them until I met you.'

'Oh, Jack.' She could feel her heart swell with love for him. She understood finally how much he'd overcome just to be able to commit to her.

'I'm not interested in other women. I like what I've got right here, what we've got together.' His free hand came up to stroke her temple.

'So do I.' She pressed her cheek to his palm.

'While I was so far away I slowly realised how precious our relationship was.' His lips quirked. 'But everything had been so final between us when I left that I spent the trip home in a cold sweat in case you'd already started divorce proceedings. Perhaps even started a relationship with someone else.'

'You're not *that* easy to get over,' she said dryly.

'Good.' He grinned, unrepentant. He lifted his arm and laid it along the back of the sofa.

'Besides,' she said, patting her stomach, 'you seriously handicapped my chances on the singles scene by leaving behind your own personal advocate.'

'Yeah, I did, didn't I?' He played with her hair, tucking a stray strand behind her ear. 'I'm a very clever man.'

'Sneaky. You're a very *sneaky* man.'

The look in his eyes brought her breathlessness back with a vengeance.

'Mmm-hmm. So where were we before we got side-tracked?'

'We were in the bedroom.' She hardly recognised her voice as the words croaked out. 'Shall we go back there?'

'I think we should.'

CHAPTER THIRTEEN

CREATIVE abdominal acrobatics jolted Liz awake in the small hours the next morning. The room was awash with light from the full moon. She lay for a moment, half-asleep, looking at the familiar bedside scene.

Something was different.

She *felt* different. Smug. Whole.

A movement in the bed behind her brought memories of the evening flooding back.

Jack.

Her lips curved as she stretched lightly. He'd always been a considerate lover, wanting her enjoyment and satisfaction as much as his own. But last night he'd been so gentle, so tender with her that she'd felt infinitely precious. His care warmed her heart, filled her with love for him. And the memory of his hands, clever and compelling, on her skin sent her system buzzing all over again. He knew her, knew what worked for her, what made her body clamour for the magic of his touch.

Thank goodness for the prenatal class. To think she'd been *afraid* it would be a catalyst for dramatic change to their relationship. And the change *had* been dramatic, but it'd been the very best thing that could have happened to them.

Falling asleep with Jack's arms around her had been the

sweetest experience. He was a haven to her, safety and security. She felt ready to tackle anything with him at her side. Even if he couldn't bring himself to lavish affection on their daughter, to bond with her, Liz knew she would be able to cope as a parent if she had his support. He was a man who could be relied on.

She rolled over to face him. A moonbeam cut a swathe through the open curtains, giving her a clear view of him. He lay on his back with his face turned towards her. His eyelashes fanned out in two dark crescents. Her gaze was drawn to his mouth, soft in repose, deliciously wicked when kissing hers. Stubble shadowed his cheeks and tussled spikes of hair framed his forehead.

He made her feel so special, cherished.

He made her feel *safe*.

But only months ago she'd been so close to losing him. She'd convinced herself she was ready to let him go, to let their love die. Her heart squeezed hard. If he hadn't been so determined to stay and try to make their marriage work, how very different her life would be now.

How very different her future would be looking.

His strength and courage had saved something precious.

If his fiancée had allowed herself to be swayed by his determination all those years ago, he'd have been married to someone else. Liz shivered. She would never have experienced loving him.

He'd been nonchalant about the long-ago affair, but she could still hear the echo of his heartbreak for the baby. And maybe for his fiancée's callous betrayal. Hadn't Kylie understood what a treasure she'd caught?

But she must have. She'd instinctively turned to Jack—not her other lover—when she'd discovered her pregnancy. Choosing him as the best partner for her future, the best potential father for her baby.

Poor Jack. First his mother, then his first love had proved to be fickle creatures. With such a background, it was a wonder he'd leapt so precipitously into marriage. Though maybe the very spur-of-the-moment nature of his proposal while they'd been on holiday together in New Zealand was the only way he could have done it. If he'd given it more thought, would they be married?

'Hey, gorgeous,' said a husky voice. 'What's up?'

'Your daughter's early morning callisthenics.'

He rolled onto his side to face her, his hand finding her stomach to stroke it softly. He opened his eyes properly. 'So she's gone back to sleep and you can't?'

'Mmm. I was just thinking.'

'I can see that.' He smiled, the moonlight glinting off his teeth. His eyelids drifted down. 'Should I be worried?'

'Jack?'

'Hmm?'

'Why did you marry me?'

His eyes blinked open wide. 'Bloody hell, Liz. What sort of question is that for…' he raised his head and squinted at the clock '…three o'clock in the morning?' His arms reached out and pulled her closer. 'There are much better things to do.'

'Really? Like what?'

'Mmm.' He nibbled on her ear. 'Kiss and cuddle for a start.'

'You're trying to distract me,' she said a few minutes later when his lips released hers.

'Mmm-hmm. Guilty.' He sighed. 'But obviously not doing a very good job of it.'

'Pretty good.' She shivered as his fingers trailed over her sternum. 'But I still want to know.'

He nuzzled her ear and his hand settled over her breast, fondling gently as though to punctuate his statement. 'Marrying you seemed to be the best way to have my lustful way with you whenever I wanted to.'

'You were anyway,' she said breathlessly.

'Oh, yeah. That's right.' He chuckled, a lovely rumbling sound vibrating in her ear. After a moment, he said, 'Then it must have been because you swept me off my feet while we were on holiday.'

'You always did have a convenient memory. The way I remember it, *you* did the sweeping.'

He drew back and looked at her seriously for a long moment. 'Perhaps I recognised my destiny as soon as I laid eyes on you and didn't see any reason to fight it.'

'Love at first sight, you mean?'

His palm curved over her cheek, his thumb rubbing her bottom lip. 'Yeah. That.'

Her heart skipped a beat. *Yes, but what about now?* Was it still love that held him to her? Or duty? She knew he had a strong sense of duty and she hated the thought that it might be his main reason for staying.

'And you didn't need me. That was a hell of a turn-on.' He rolled onto his back and gathered her close to his side. 'I *wanted* to look after you. And I hadn't wanted to do that for anyone for years. Your independence was a challenge. And a relief.'

'After Janet?'

'Mmm. And Kylie. You were busy getting on with your life. You didn't need a partner to make you whole.' He slid his free hand under his head. 'My relationships were short and shallow until I met you.'

'Left a trail of broken hearts, did you?' She ran her fingers across his chest, enjoying the texture against her palm.

'Not fair. I was always up front at the start of my relationships.'

'Big of you.' She lightly tugged a few of the hairs. 'So why didn't you warn me?'

He grunted, capturing her playful fingers. 'You weren't the one who needed warning, I was. Why'd you agree to marry me?'

'Um. Lots of reasons. I've always liked a man in uniform and you do fill yours out very nicely. And I was enjoying having my lustful way with you. And you proposed to me so romantically.' She smiled, remembering the holiday madness. 'It was crazy. Spontaneous. You were magic and you made me feel as though *I* could be fun.'

'Hey, darlin'. Trust me, you are,' he growled suggestively.

'Then there was the fact that I loved you.' She swallowed, gathering her courage and tilting her head on his shoulder so she could look him in the face. 'I still do.'

'Oh, Liz. I love you, too.'

'Thank you,' she whispered, blinking away the sudden rush of moisture in her eyes. 'I've needed to hear that so much.'

'Hey, all you had to do was ask. You're everything a bloke could want in a sheila.'

She chuckled, feeling the urge to cry recede. 'You're such a romantic, Jack Campbell.'

'I know.'

'I mean it.' Liz pushed herself up on her elbow and looked down at him. 'I found the airline tickets. Why didn't you tell me?'

'We had more important things to work out.' He looked uncomfortable.

'I'd love to go back to New Zealand.'

'We can.' He rubbed his hand over her shoulder. Liz couldn't suppress a small shiver at his touch. 'When Emma's old enough, we will.'

'I'd like that. A second honeymoon.'

'Mmm-hmm. Now, go back to sleep. Roll over so we can snuggle.'

He curved his body around hers. She could feel the roughness of his chest hair against her shoulder blades. His muscular legs bent against the backs of hers, his exhalations fanning the nape of her neck. She could hear his breathing slow as he drifted off. Sleep claimed her as she was thinking how delicious the sensations of having him close were.

A feather-light caress on her lips woke her the next morning and she opened her eyes to find Jack leaning over her.

'Mmm. Prince Charming, I presume.' She reached up, sinking her fingers into his hair, pulling his head down. His lips moved warmly over hers, knowing all the spots she liked to be touched. Varying the pressure, light and teasing one moment, firm and thorough the next. Powerful, skilful caresses that she'd missed in the months he'd been away. And missed even more poignantly in the weeks he'd been home, so near and yet so far. His touch felt right, perfect for her.

He drew her arms away from his neck and held her hands pinned to the bed above her head, finishing the kiss with a light nip of her bottom lip.

'Stop it, Dr Campbell, or I'm going to have to come back to bed.'

'What's stopping you?' She shifted, her fingers curling helplessly in his grip.

'I'm being considerate.' He leaned in to give her another quick peck before releasing her and standing up. 'Now, I'm going for a run to work off some of this excess energy you've left me with.'

'I can think of something else that might help.'

'You're a wicked woman, Liz, my love. But I'm not undoing all the rest you've had by wearing you out in bed the first chance I get. I do have *some* self-control.'

'Too much.' She tried a pout.

'Sorry. Gorgeous though you look, pouting is not going to work.'

Liz watched him walk to the door, enjoying the sight of his broad shoulders and long, lean back. His Lycra running shorts showed off his taut backside and the flex of well-toned muscles.

'Nice buns.'

'Glad you think so.' He flashed her a grin and was gone. His voice floated back to her. 'I'll fix you breakfast when I get home.'

Liz sighed and fell back on the pillows for a few extra lazy moments.

Everything was perfect.

Perfect.

Jack still loved her. Still wanted her physically even though she was enormously pregnant. He was talking to her more than he ever had before. Their marriage was back on track. He might not actively *want* to be a father, but he was going to be here to support her.

So why did she feel uneasy? Was it just her pregnancy mood swings making her feel this way? Surely she wasn't turning into one of those difficult people who didn't allow anything to please them. Maybe it was just that their reconciliation was so new she was a little uncertain about it? All she needed was time to adjust to this new reality. That was reasonable, wasn't it?

But her uneasiness hadn't abated over the following week, Liz acknowledged silently as they drove to the hospital for the next class.

She'd covered it up as best she could, not wanting to make Jack think he was failing her in any way at all. Because he wasn't. He'd been brilliant.

She didn't want him to think she was impossible to please. He'd spoken of her independence being one of the things he loved. Lord, if he knew how she was feeling right now he'd be terrified. She'd never been like this before. What was wrong with her?

She couldn't talk to him about her nebulous anxiety. How could she say to him, *I'm not happy, but I don't know why?* No, until she could pinpoint the problem, she couldn't dump it on him.

But perhaps she could talk about other things. Maybe finding out how Jack felt would make her feel better.

'It's the last class tonight,' she said as he parked the car at the hospital.

'Mmm.'

'Scary, isn't it?' She tried to sound casual, but perhaps she hadn't succeeded because she could feel his gaze on her. 'Just think, after this we're supposed to know what we're doing.'

'Yeah. Worried?'

She sighed and turned her head to look at him. 'Yes, I am. Not about the birth,' she said quickly when he opened his mouth to speak. 'About after. About actually being a parent. Aren't you?'

'Yes. And no.' He smiled as he captured her hand. 'I know you're going to be a great mum so I figure if I take my cue from you, I can't go wrong.'

She felt a lump forming in her throat. 'You're a very sweet man, Jack.'

'Sweet?' He sounded disgusted.

'Mmm. It's a side of you I haven't seen before. Why is that?'

'Perhaps you've never needed me to be sweet before.' He squeezed her hand then opened his door. By the time she'd got herself organised to get out of the car he was waiting to help her.

She clambered out awkwardly, pausing for a moment to arch her lower back.

'Sore?'

'No worse than usual.'

'I'll give you a massage later.'

'Sounds good.' She loved his hands on her, couldn't get enough of his touch. They hadn't made love as often as she'd thought they might. He seemed concerned about the baby. She should appreciate his consideration.

And she did. Much as she craved his closeness, her advanced pregnancy was making her tired.

She waddled beside him, feeling slow and cumbersome. He shortened his long strides to accommodate her pace, making her even more aware of her lack of grace.

'It's when she thinks she's ready to date that scares me,' he murmured as they reached the classroom. 'Will Julie be giving lessons on that?'

Liz chuckled, her tension unwinding a fraction. As long as they could keep their sense of humour, everything would be all right, wouldn't it?

After they'd done the relaxation and exercises, Julie brought out her dummy babies and announced the next segment.

Nappies 101.

Liz's unease returned in full force as she watched Jack. Through the general hilarity around the table, she could see his long fingers competently folding the square cloth in thirds, making the thick pad, pulling out the flaps to pin.

'Don't worry too much,' said the midwife to reassure the struggling partners. 'You'll all get plenty of practice. Your baby will need about ten changes a day. That adds up to more than three thousand nappies in the first year.'

But Liz could see that Jack needed no practice. He wrapped the nappy around his dummy's legs and pinned the flaps in place as the others fumbled their way through the exercise.

The line of men held their 'babies' up. The nappies of all the first-time fathers promptly dropped to the table.

Except Jack's.

His was snug and tidy.

Perfect.

And unbelievably threatening.

'Oh, dear. Look at Pete's disaster,' groaned one of the other mothers-to-be. 'Perhaps Jack could come over and give him some lessons.'

Liz managed a smile, hoping it didn't look as sickly as it felt.

Jack was better at this than she was. He must have done even more for his little sister than he'd led her to believe. Would she feel better if he was as ham-fisted as some of the other new fathers? Surely she couldn't be that small-minded and competitive. Could she?

But *why* wasn't she pleased? Intellectually, she could see that she should be ecstatic, but somewhere deep in her psyche it all felt wrong.

Wrong that he was so competent.

Wrong that she was so disturbed about it.

Was she worried he would watch her handling their newborn and find her wanting? After all, he'd judged his mother harshly.

Liz sighed. She wasn't being fair. Janet had deserved to be judged and if anyone had a right to do it, that person was her own child. The son she'd ultimately deserted because her habit had been stronger than her love.

'You're very quiet,' said Jack on the drive home.

'Am I?' She roused herself from her troubled thoughts and glanced at him briefly. 'I'm tired.'

'That's all?'

'Yes.'

'We're nearly home.'

'You starred in the class tonight.' She winced at the accusing tone. Trying to lighten the mood, she added, 'Perhaps you need to give me some lessons. On nappies. And, um, babies.'

That sounded worse.

She shifted uncomfortably. 'Um. So your, um, expertise, is that because of your little sister?'

'Yeah. I was Emma's live-in babysitter.'

'Janet was lucky to have you, wasn't she?'

Jack didn't bother to answer her and in the lengthening silence Liz knew she'd been unreasonable.

'I—I'm sorry, Jack. That wasn't very nice,' she said in a

low voice. 'I'm cranky and I don't really understand why. But that's no reason to take it out on you.'

'Don't worry about it, darlin', I've got broad shoulders.' His hand covered hers, the hard palm warm against her cold fingers.

'Well, don't be too nice to me or I'll be crying all over them.' Tears flooded her eyes. With the back of her hand, she wiped the droplets that spilled onto her cheeks.

'You're just tired. I know you haven't been sleeping very well. Only four weeks to go now.'

'*Only*? Twenty-eight *whole* days.' It was a relief to let the words explode out of her, sweeping away the need to cry. 'I don't know how I'm going to do it, Jack. I feel ready to burst now.'

'My poor darling.'

'You're being nice to me again.' She sniffed. 'I know most women say they feel the same way at this stage.'

'But it's different when it's you?'

'Yes, it is. Damn it.' She chuckled softly. 'I want to cringe when I think of all the words of wisdom I've imparted to my pregnant patients over the years. What did I know?'

Later that night, Jack lay listening to Liz's soft, steady breathing. She'd dropped off to sleep quickly, but he knew the chances were she'd be awake again in a few hours.

Tonight's antenatal class had been interesting. He was surprised and pleased how easily his old knowledge had come back to him. It'd been fun—though he'd had to endure the good-natured teasing of the other men.

What hadn't been so good was Liz's reaction to his expertise. He'd seen her face as he'd held up his diapered dummy and she'd looked…stricken was the best word he could think of. He'd expected her to be pleased, felt hurt that she wasn't.

She'd managed to dredge up a smile when Pete McGill's wife had leaned over to speak to her, but he could tell it had been an effort.

And he definitely hadn't imagined it. Her snippy comments on the way home confirmed that. So what was wrong?

He'd thought their problems had been sorted out when he'd come round to the idea of fatherhood. But peeling away that issue seemed to have exposed something he was at a loss to explain. And Liz didn't seem inclined to even try, passing her comments off as pregnancy crankiness. And this was the first time she'd really complained about the way she felt so perhaps that's all it was.

He worried about her, the pace at which she drove herself. He loved her independence, but sometimes it would be nice if she would lean on him. Just a little.

She rolled towards him, her hand sliding across his stomach and hooking around his waist. He sucked in a breath sharply as he felt his body react to her touch. At least they seemed to have ironed out the problems in *this* area of their relationship. Even if he did have to set a much more restrained pace than his natural inclination. He was close to her, sleeping with her. Loving her. They could sort everything else out as they went along. For now, this was a start.

He caught her hand as it strayed lower and she murmured a protest in her sleep. Letting out a long, slow lungful of air, he held her hand flat to his chest and took firm rein on his lust.

She needed sleep. She needed sleep.

He grinned wryly.

And *he* deserved a damned medal.

CHAPTER FOURTEEN

'I THOUGHT you had the day off today.' Jack stopped in the bedroom doorway, surprised to see Liz up and dressed.

'I have, but I wanted to get around to visit a few people.' She sounded distracted as she bent to pull up the bedspread. 'Sort of tidy up loose ends.'

'I've got this.' He twitched the heavy cover out of her hands and flung it up the bed. 'Like who? Can't it wait?'

'No, it can't wait. Look, if you're going to make the bed, you need to do it properly.'

'Liz.' He reached out and stopped her from straightening the bedclothes. 'I'll do that in a minute. I know you didn't sleep well again last night. You should take the opportunity to rest today. Where are you going that's so all fired important?'

'Oh, I try not to disturb you when I get up.' She looked at him guiltily. 'I'm sorry.'

He shrugged. 'I've heard you a couple of times, that's all. Where are you going today?'

'I want to see how Uncle Ron's doing.'

'Hell, Liz. The McLeods live miles out of town.' He scowled down at her, seeing the bluish shadows beneath her eyes, the pale cheeks. The blooming good health she usually projected seemed to have faded overnight. 'Why can't I take you out there next weekend?'

'I haven't been out there for a couple of weeks. Besides, it's not that far. And it's not just them. I—I thought I might pop in and see Mum. If I have time.' Her eyes slid away from his, making him wonder what she wasn't telling him.

'There's no reason why I can't take you *there* next weekend, too,' he said, hard pressed to keep his tone neutral. Visiting Patrice... Not something he'd look forward to. Unfortunately, the only thing Liz's mother and he agreed on was their mutual dislike for each other. Patrice believed her daughter had married beneath her station.

Liz's face lit up with a cheeky grin, her hazel eyes twinkling at him. 'Hmm, you must love me. Thank you, darling. I appreciate your offer, but I won't do it to you.' She sobered. 'I—I haven't arranged anything with Mum.'

'You're just going to drop in? On Patrice? Feeling masochistic, sweetheart?'

'I didn't want her making a big fuss.' She braced her lower back and arched slightly. 'I thought if I just called in that we could just have an informal chat about...some things.'

'Why would you think that? It's never worked in the past.' He swallowed his frustration, not wanting to badger her.

'I know. I thought...hoped today might be different.' She looked so forlorn he couldn't bring himself to say any more on the matter. But his instinct to protect was on high alert. If Patrice gave Liz a hard time, she'd answer to him.

'Sure.' He held out his arms. 'Come here and let me do that for you.'

Liz came so willingly to him that his heart swelled with love.

He gripped her hips, digging his thumbs into the muscles at the top of her buttocks. She moaned softly.

'Too hard?'

'No. Too good.' She sighed and rested her forehead on his shoulder.

He smiled and laid his cheek on her hair as he continued

the rhythmic kneading. His petite wife was a real trouper, suffering the discomforts of her pregnancy with quiet dignity. Mostly her lack of complaint was because of the type of person she was. But he was sure part of it was because of his initial resistance to starting a family. She didn't want to bother him. Although he'd done his best to reassure her since he'd come home from the States, he had the feeling she wasn't entirely convinced he was going to stay.

How she could doubt him was a mystery. Didn't she realise she was part of him? He'd be lost without her in his life. She'd rescued him from his superficial, love-'em-and-leave-'em roundabout, given him a richness he couldn't begin to put a value on.

Hopefully, time would take care of her uncertainty. In the meantime, he would have to take care of her. As much as she'd let him.

Liz wasn't absolutely sure why she hadn't forewarned her mother of her intention to visit. She'd told Jack she wanted it to be informal, which was true. But as she drove through town, she wondered if she might be hoping the short notice would surprise a genuine response from her buttoned-up parent.

Twenty minutes later, Liz pulled up in her mother's driveway and turned off the ignition. Doubts crowded in now that she was here. Was she really prepared for this confrontation? The problem with surprising people was that you didn't always get the results you expected...or wanted.

She sat for long moments, examining the clean lines of her mother's formal garden. Beautiful but untouchable. Tiny hedges perfectly trimmed into geometric patterns, plants chosen for size and colour. And tractability. They were *yes* plants.

Her mother had tried to trim and prune her offspring into shape with secateurs of carefully meted-out doses of affection and approval.

But children weren't passive botanical specimens. She and her younger brother had burst out in unexpected directions. Mark, the heir destined to carry the Dustin name, refused to grow up, refused to marry, instead regularly throwing himself into the path of danger with his extreme sports.

Liz's own rebellion had been more subtle, starting with her career and then her marriage to Jack with his working-class Scottish background. But choosing him hadn't been a deliberate act of mutiny. She'd laid eyes on him and wanted him immediately. Still did. She was lucky—he'd wanted her right back.

But while that seemed to be a reasonable basis for a relationship, did it work for a marriage? Even more important, was it a good foundation to be parents?

They'd both had examples of what not to do, especially Jack with his drug-addicted mother. Janet's behaviour had been patently flawed.

But Liz was beginning to wonder if her own family issues were more insidious. On the surface, she'd had a stable upbringing with both parents. But her father had provided the necessities—no more. Her mother, on the other hand, had done all the *right* things and had been seen to do them.

It dawned on her that her parents had never been a team. Never united through any of the domestic crises. Never made any spontaneous gestures of affection or support toward each other.

Perhaps that's what she'd reacted to as a child, what she'd missed in her family. And why she'd craved acknowledgment from her parents, especially her father. He'd never said he loved her, that he was proud of her. She'd have done anything to wring some emotion from him other than indifference.

Was her drive to make Jack prove he'd be a caring father a result of the separateness she'd sensed in her parents' marriage?

She needed to understand the emotional core of her family. But how did she find the right questions to ask? All she knew was some instinct had driven her here today to make the effort. If she didn't, she might be doomed to repeating the patterns with her own children. And that was unacceptable.

Liz rubbed her hand over her stomach. She mustn't make the same mistakes. Love had to be unconditional. Her own behaviour had to change. She'd begun to realise how conditional she'd made her love for Jack. First on having children, then by trying to dictate the type of father he'd be.

Gathering her bag, she pushed open the door. She had to deal with one thing at a time. Right now, she'd find out about her family.

She stood for a moment beside the car, rubbing her lower back. The beneficial effects of Jack's massage had worn off and the muscles felt tired and achy.

'Elizabeth.'

'Hello, Mum.' Liz turned to face the owner of the cool voice.

'This is a surprise.' A small, unsmiling silence that spoke volumes.

Liz could feel herself wanting to retreat, wishing she hadn't come. Bracing herself, she kept her smile blandly pleasant. 'I was passing so I thought I'd drop in.'

'I saw you sitting in the car. I was beginning to think you weren't going to come in.'

Liz wondered how long her mother had been watching. Had she been hoping her daughter would just drive away?

'You're lucky you caught me home.' Patrice stripped off her gardening gloves, plucking each finger forcefully.

'Are you on your way out, Mum?'

'No. But I might have been and then you'd have had a wasted trip. You'd better come in.'

Her mother led the way through to the back of the house. Liz followed slowly, walking past the familiar rooms with an odd sense of detachment. Everything was formal, spotless, rigidly tidy and decorated in pale colours that showed every

mark from tiny grubby fingers. Even the carpet had pile designed to show every scuff from small running feet. Nothing
had been changed for years. Hard to believe two children had
grown up in this house.

Liz realised her arm had curled protectively over her pregnant stomach.

'Would you like something to drink?'

The discouraging tone nearly made Liz smile.

'Don't make anything especially.' She propped herself on
the stool by the bench to give her tired legs a quick rest. Today
was obviously going to be a physically difficult one. 'I'm on
my way out to the McLeods' place.' Liz could have bitten her
tongue.

'I see.' Her mother washed and dried her hands before
asking, 'And how are Ronald and Margaret?'

'Aunty Peg's a Trojan. And Uncle Ron's as well as can
be expected.'

'I don't know why you're so familiar with them, Elizabeth,'
the older woman said with distaste. 'It's not as if they're really
your family.'

'They're Jack's family, Mum, therefore they are mine. And
they treat me as part of their family so that's what counts.'
Standing firm felt good, right.

'Hmph. Well, I suppose you'll do as you see fit.' She
sniffed. 'I can't imagine what's possessed Margaret to let
Ronald stay at home at this stage of his illness. And it's
dragging on dreadfully.'

'Being at home has perked Uncle Ron up. He's decided he
wants to stay around a bit longer. There was nothing more that
we could do for him in the hospital,' said Liz, feeling obliged
to defend his decision.

'Yes, but he could have stayed there with the nurses to look
after him rather than expecting his wife to do it.'

'But she wants to. And they have their daughter staying as

well. She's a qualified nurse. It's what he wanted, Mum.' Though she didn't want to continue the discussion, Liz had a feeling of sick inevitability that it would lead to the questions she did want to ask. 'That's important, don't you think?'

'It hardly matters what I think, does it?'

'You'd have done the same for Dad, wouldn't you?' Liz wondered if she really believed that. Or did she just want it to be true?

'Heavens! The questions you ask, Elizabeth.' With the kettle plugged in, the older woman set out two mugs before arranging biscuits in a perfect fan around the edge of a plate. 'It's a moot point since your father died the way he did.'

'Yes.' Her father had had the good sense to die quickly from a massive heart attack. Tidily, barely disrupting his wife's garden club schedule. Liz pushed the treacherous thought away.

Her mother had never been a warm, affectionate woman. Liz wanted desperately to be different with her own children. But did she know how? All those years she'd studied to be a doctor, but could she learn how to nurture her daughter's spirit? Teach her to be whole and happy and independent?

Put to the test, Liz wondered if she would prove to be just as cold as her parents.

'Did Dad want children?'

'Want them? What's that got to do with anything? The Dustins were a very influential family in the area.'

'Yes, I know.' She fought to keep any hint of censure out of her voice. The family's social position had been imprinted on her throughout her childhood. But bringing it into the conversation didn't tell her what she wanted to know about her father. 'I just wondered because I don't remember him ever playing with us when we were kids. Not even with Mark.'

Or hugging us, or coming to school plays, or sports days, or even kissing us goodnight.

'Your father was a busy man.'

The answer was unsatisfactory and yet maybe it was all there was to be gleaned here. In the silence that followed, Liz swallowed her disappointment.

'I'm your mother, Elizabeth. I didn't need him to be involved. Raising you was *my* job.' The older woman looked surprised at the information she'd volunteered. She shook her head and adjusted the position of the teapot with small jerky movements.

In a moment of cold clarity, Liz suddenly understood her instinct to block Jack's involvement with their baby. If she continued, she'd ruin a potentially beautiful and loving relationship between Jack and his daughter. She'd begun to suspect her own behaviour, but to have it presented to her like this was a shock.

'No, Mum, I guess you didn't.'

But what about me? She wanted to rail against the isolation she'd felt from her father. If things had been different, would he have wanted to be involved with his children?

'Was your marriage to Dad a happy one?' Liz knew how it had looked from her point of view, but now she wanted to know how it had been from her mother's side. If her parents had believed they were happy then what did it matter how it seemed to someone else?

'Happy?' Her mother looked startled, as though the concept was completely alien.

The kettle screamed.

'Yes. Did Dad make you happy?' Even to her own ears there was a desperate quality to the question. 'You must have been in love when you got married.'

The silence stretched as Patrice spooned tea leaves into the pot and added boiling water. She kept her eyes focussed on the cups on the bench then reached out to align the handles of the cups.

Was she hoping the question would go away? Liz wondered with grim amusement.

'Mum?'

'Oh, for heaven's sake.' Her mother gave an exasperated sigh. 'Perhaps it's time you knew. What I was when I got married, Elizabeth, was pregnant.'

'Yes, I know, but—'

'How do you know?' Her mother's face flushed and then went chalky white. 'I never told you. Your father certainly wouldn't have told you.'

'Simple arithmetic. I worked it out in high school. But surely…that's not why you got married?'

Her mother's mouth pinched unattractively.

Liz's heart lurched as she tried again. 'Well, not the only reason. Mum?'

'It's really none of your business.'

'Well, yes, I think it might be my business,' said Liz slowly. 'We were never a cosy, loving family and I need to understand why not. You see, that's what I want for my child. A cosy, loving family.'

Her mother glared at her. 'Children need discipline and stability, not wishy-washy sentiments.'

'I think they need both.' She thought again of Jack's traumatic upbringing and what he'd had to conquer to become the man she'd married. 'I think they especially need to know they're loved and wanted for themselves.'

'Are you telling me your father and I didn't do a good job of bringing you up?' Patrice's voice was scratchy and high with tension.

'No, I'm—'

'You and your brother are both well-educated adults. And you have a useful career, don't you? One that *you* wanted.' Knuckles gleamed whitely in her mother's clenched fists. 'Who was it who put you through medical school and made that possible?'

'You and Dad. But—'

'You're very lucky, aren't you, Elizabeth? With your doting husband and your career and now your tidy little pregnancy and plans. It will be interesting to see how you juggle your precious career and marriage once you have a child.'

Liz took in a shaky breath, feeling the fine tremors in her muscles from the adrenalin charging around her system. She seemed to have pushed her mother into uncharacteristic candour. The brutal honesty of the words was exposing so many of her own fears that Liz quailed momentarily. But if she wanted to know anything, now was the time to ask.

She met her mother's eyes across the bench. 'You didn't want children? You and Dad? Was Dad angry when you got pregnant?'

'Don't be naive, Elizabeth. Your father was a lot like you. He was fond of tidy little plans, too. I ruined them.'

'But attitudes towards pregnancy weren't so dogmatic then, were they?' Liz forced the words out of her dry mouth. 'Didn't you both have other options?'

'Your father was a Dustin in a country town named after his forebears, Elizabeth. His mother made sure he did the right thing. There was no other option.'

'I see. I—I don't think I'll have time for that cup of tea after all, Mum.' Liz managed a tight smile. 'I'll see myself out.'

She was running away. Her system felt battered by the confrontation. Emotional pain lanced through her with such strength that it manifested physically, leaving her so nauseous that her abdomen ached. She'd judged Jack unprepared for parenthood but suddenly her own inadequacy seemed insurmountable.

Her hand trembled as she slotted the key into the ignition. She wanted to go home, curl up on the bed and forget the morning.

More than anything she wanted Jack. But how could she turn to him right now? She'd trapped him as surely as her mother had trapped her father. The enormity of what she'd done would overwhelm any comfort she might derive from his reassurance. What hope did the future hold for them with these handicaps from the past?

She drove slowly, glad of the concentration demanded by the winding road through to the McLeods' property. Aunty Peg's undisciplined garden seemed to tumble across the ground to greet her as she pulled up in the driveway.

She sat for a moment, enjoying the sprawling friendliness before scrambling out of the car with her bag.

'Liz!' A large elderly woman in overalls hurried along the path towards her. A moment later Liz was enveloped in a huge hug from Jack's great-aunt.

'Aunty Peg.' The warm welcome brought quick tears to her eyes.

'It's grand to see you.' The woman stepped back and held her at arm's length. 'You're looking bonnie as usual, lass. A little peaky mebbe. Is that grandnephew of mine looking after you now? He was up here last week, organising his boys to do some burning off for us. But what're you doing way out here with this storm brewing? I've just had Jack on the phone, trying to find you.'

For the first time Liz became aware of the iron-grey clouds boiling across the sky. She suppressed a shiver. How had she not noticed the change earlier? Had it so matched her dark mood she'd been oblivious?

'Och, and here's me not taking a breath so you can answer me. Come through and see Ron. Have you time to have a brew with us, then?'

'That would be lovely.' Bag in hand, she walked up the path with the elderly woman.

'How have you been feeling?'

'I'm slowing down, Aunty Peg.'

'Little wonder. It can't be long now.'

'Another three weeks.'

'That long? I'd be surprised. The babe's dropped. Och, but you don't need me to tell you that.'

'I think this will definitely be my last visit before the baby comes.' She rested her hand on her stomach.

'Aye. I think so, too.' Aunty Peg ushered her into the small cluttered entrance. Delicious smells of fresh baking greeted them. 'Go through to the lounge, Liz. I just need to wash up.'

Liz walked down the dark, narrow hallway and paused in the lounge doorway a moment to appreciate the view out the huge picture window that dominated the room. Stormclouds shrouded the hills, blocking the usual view of the distant mountains.

'Ron!' bellowed Aunty Peg from the other end of the hall. 'Look who's come to see you, then.'

A gnome-like face appeared around the edge of a recliner.

'Lizzie! How's my favourite doctor?'

'I'm good, Uncle Ron. How's my favourite patient?'

'Top of the world, lass. I feel like an auld fraud with everyone's fussing.'

'Since I'm here I might as well check you over.' Liz methodically ran through her examination. Focussing on the routine task restored her equilibrium and she was delighted to find Jack's great-uncle much better than expected.

'You're getting plenty of rest?' She packed up her gear as Aunty Peg pushed the tea trolley into the room.

'Och, why would I want to be doing that, Lizzie, lass? Plenty of time for that.' His lined face wrinkled into a puckish grin. 'Got to enjoy life while I can, don't I?'

'You do.' She popped a kiss on his forehead.

Liz sat, enjoying a cup of tea, listening to the gentle banter between the couple.

'It's our fifty-third wedding anniversary next month,' said Ron.

'Och, she knows that. Do you no' remember she met our Jack at our fiftieth?'

'So I did.' Liz looked at the beaming faces of her unlikely cupids. Did she and Jack have the staying power to see such a milestone in their marriage?

Jack. Suddenly, she wanted the hug she'd felt so undeserving of after her visit with her mother.

'I'd better go.' She put her cup on the coffee table. Bracing her back, she stood carefully, huffing out a breath at the discomfort that caused her lower body.

'Liz, are you sure you should be driving, lass? Can I no' ring Jack and get him to come for you?'

'No, thanks, Aunty Peg. It'll only take me a bit over half an hour to get home.'

'Och, closer to an hour. But I suppose there's no arguing with you, is there? There's a box on your passenger seat with eggs and fresh veggies. I've put a parcel of nappies there as well from my last grandchild. They're all freshly laundered for you. And there's a wee present for the bairn, lass,' the elderly woman said as they walked out to the vehicle.

'Oh, thank you, Aunty Peg. You're very kind. I should open it before I go.'

'No, you should not. Unless you'll change your mind and let me get that bonnie man of yours up here to take care of you.'

Liz hesitated briefly, but some instinct was pushing her on. She had to get to Jack. She needed him. Waiting didn't feel right. She had to keep moving.

CHAPTER FIFTEEN

JACK paced to the open doors of the station. Banks of sullen, charcoal clouds pressed down over the hills. Wispy fingers of dingy grey trailed threateningly towards the earth. The atmosphere was oppressive and still.

Behind him the tankers were ready to go, crouched on the concrete floor of the shed. But it was unlikely they were going to be needed today with the high humidity.

He spun on his heel and strode back into the station.

'Any calls?'

'Nup.' Danny looked up from the sports section of the newspaper. 'Not since you asked five minutes ago. What's the problem?'

'Liz.' Jack sighed, feeling his frustration grow as he ran a hand down his face. 'She's gone out to visit Aunty Peg and Uncle Ron. She wanted to do it before the baby arrives.'

He stalked over to the large wall map. His eyes traced the winding road around the terrain contours to the McLeods' from Patrice's place, picturing in his mind the lowest points. The road was almost a private one through to the McLeods' and then not much more than a fire track after that. The only other dwelling was Ernie Thomas's weekend shack about halfway between the two gullies. If the storm broke while Liz was out there…

Where the hell was she?

And *how* was she?

The last couple of weeks had been tough for her. She'd been grumpy and trying so hard not to show it. Didn't she think he could take it? He smiled tightly. Compared to his mother in a savage mood, Liz was a honey.

He knew she was struggling physically, not sleeping properly. He'd been waking regularly to find her wandering the house. He knew she tried hard not to disturb him. And she didn't. A sort of sixth sense alerted him when she wasn't in bed. He'd offered to sleep in the spare room again if it'd make it easier for her to rest, but she'd been adamant that she didn't want him to move. He'd been gratified to know she wanted him close. Because that's exactly where he wanted to be.

'Give her a ring,' said Danny, interrupting his thoughts.

'I've tried.' Several times. He'd tried Aunty Peg as well, but the line had been engaged. He turned away from the map. 'Her mobile's out of range or turned off.'

He'd got through to her mother, spoken to the charming Patrice. He knew approximately what time Liz had left there. She should be well and truly at Aunty Peg's by now. Maybe even on her way back.

But what sort of mood had she been in after visiting her mother? Patrice had been typically unhelpful. Though he had learned that Liz had been asking questions. Personal, impertinent ones that had definitely ruffled his usually cool, controlled mother-in-law.

So, how was Liz?

Jack hated the thought of her running around the countryside upset after a confrontation. He cursed himself for not taking more notice of her distraction that morning. She'd seemed uncertain, almost…guilty? Had she been planning then to tackle her mother about those *personal questions*? If so, he had the feeling that she'd already begun doubting the wisdom of her intentions.

He checked his watch again. Great. Another ten minutes had passed.

His adorable, dedicated, serious wife wasn't the sort to take stupid chances. But perhaps the scene with her mother meant she hadn't been thinking clearly. Add that to her advanced pregnancy and lack of sleep—she needed to be cared for, damn it, and he had the growing sense he was failing to do that.

He huffed out an impatient breath and glared at the map again as if that might help him see her location. The impotence of not knowing where she was, how she was, drove him crazy. If there was no problem, he was going to throttle her when he got hold of her for worrying him like this.

Enough. He wasn't going to hang around wondering what the hell was happening. He'd try Aunty Peg's number again and then he was going out to hunt for Liz. The phone in his office rang as he reached for it. He snatched it up.

'Dustin Fire Station.'

'Jack?'

'Aunty Peg. Is Liz there?' Jack was aware of the station radio crackling into life in the room behind him.

'That's what I wanted to talk to you about, Jack.' It was a measure of his great-aunt's anxiety that she didn't chip him about his abrupt greeting. His own sense of dread rocketed higher. 'She left here a wee while ago and I've no' been able to raise her at home. It's been teeming down for the last half an hour. I've been trying to get our Ian, but he's away up the hill. You know what those gullies on our road can be like in the wet. She's no' long to go now till the bairn and I'm worried about her. No' that she was compleenin', but I thought she seemed a bit poorly. She's a stubborn wee thing, your darlin' wife.'

'She is,' he said grimly. 'I'm on my way.'

'Och, that'd be a load off my mind. I'll no' keep you, then. Let us know when you've found her.'

'I will, Aunty Peg. Thanks.' He cut the connection and punched in the number for the station's stand-by volunteer.

'Jack?' Danny appeared in the doorway, a sheaf of papers in hand, his face creased with concern. 'Didn't you say Liz has gone up to the McLeods' place?'

'Yes.'

'A flash flood warning has just come through for that whole area.' He glanced at the papers again. 'Supercell activity has caused big dumps in the high country. And the system's coming this way so we're in for a hammering.'

'Right, thanks.'

Danny hovered in the doorway as Jack outlined the situation and his plans to the volunteer.

'Bill's on his way in.' Jack tried Liz's mobile number one last time as he spoke. No reply. He crashed the receiver back into the cradle. His wife was going to be the death of him.

'Yep, no problems. We can hold the fort.' Still talking, Danny followed him out of the station house. 'Don't you worry about anything this end. Go and find your missus.'

'Thanks.' Jack slid behind the wheel of his vehicle.

'Stay in touch and let us know if we can do anything.' Danny shut the door, his fingers gripping the sill of the four-wheel drive's open window for a moment as his face screwed into a grimace. With a quick hard nod, Danny released the door. 'Good luck, mate. You just bring her home safe.'

'I will,' Jack vowed.

A malignant yellow glow tinged the early afternoon light as Jack drove through town. He was just passing Patrice's place when rain started lashing the car. It got steadily worse as he travelled closer to the hills.

He'd feel like an idiot if he battled his way up to the McLeods' and Liz was tucked up at home with a good book.

But a deep, primal urge pushed him on to find her. His mate was in peril and he had to forge his way to her side.

Hunching forward, he drove with grim concentration, negotiating the winding road as quickly as he dared. The wipers worked hard to sweep away the water sluicing across the windscreen.

No sign of Liz. He'd been half expecting, half hoping to find her broken down at the side of the road.

At last, Green Gully. Murky brown water swirled sluggishly across the road. A huge gum tree, which had fallen into the gully downstream, slowed the current. He stopped at the edge, staring across the expanse as he reviewed what he knew of the road. As he watched, he was dismayed to see the level rise unmistakably. If he was going to cross, it had to be soon.

He swore softly. Where the hell was Liz? Had she already crossed? At least it appeared she hadn't tried to get through here while the level was high. The hand he lifted to wipe his face shook slightly, making him realise just how afraid for her he was.

The rain stopped, suddenly giving him clearer view in the rapidly dimming light.

He had to go.

Now.

Slotting the vehicle into four-wheel drive, he took a deep breath and released the handbrake. The vehicle rolled slowly forward and began the painstaking crawl through the water. He could feel the tug on the steering as the pressure of the current pushed against the panels. Using all his self-discipline, he kept the engine revs constant. The temptation to hurry was nearly irresistible.

His heart lurched and his hands tightened on the wheel as the rear slewed slowly sideways. A split second later the front wheels gained traction and he began to climb the slope at the other side.

Once clear of the water, he stopped and exhaled the breath he hadn't realised he'd been holding. Liz's sedan wouldn't have coped with this sort of treatment at all.

Where was she?

He was committed now. There'd be no way back for hours with the way the water level rose behind him. If she wasn't on this road, he had to accept he'd be isolated for no good reason.

His vehicle was kept well supplied for emergency situations.

But his concern was for Liz. She needed him—he knew it.

The temperature dropped steadily and thunder rumbled, deep and threatening, in the distance. The slick road ahead was littered with leaves and debris picked out by his head-lights as he wound steadily onwards.

He rounded a tight corner.

There was her car. Hazard lights flashing, rear wheel in the ditch.

His quick relief was short-lived. *No one in the driver's seat.*

Surely, she hadn't tried to walk for help in her condition. He grabbed the torch and ran across to her vehicle. The beam speared into the dark car.

She was there, kneeling on all fours on the back seat.

Thank God.

His knees were suddenly weak. He yanked open the door, heard her breathing coming in small puffing sounds. She wasn't aware of him at all.

'Liz?' He touched her shoulder.

Her head shot up.

'Jack? Oh, God. Jack!' A few ragged sobs escaped before she grabbed control of her breathing again.

She reached out to latch onto his hand. He winced as her fingers gripped the tips of his. Even in the subdued light he could see her delicate knuckles standing out, white and bony.

His heart sank. *She was in labour.* Thoughts crowded in.

How long had she been out here, alone and in pain? Wasn't it too soon for her to have the baby? What had she said this morning? Three weeks to go? He did a quick calculation. Thirty-seven weeks. Hadn't Julie said normal delivery could happen any time after that?

But out here, in the middle of nowhere…

He swallowed.

'How long have you been in labour, darlin'?' he asked when she sagged back against the seat.

'I'm not sure. I've been feeling rotten all day.' Tears rolled down her cheeks. 'Backache and nausea. But I thought it was other things. I didn't realise it was the baby. Oh, God, Jack. I've been so stupid.'

'No, you haven't, sweetheart.' He kept his voice level, soothing. The last thing Liz needed was to see the panic surging through him. He slipped into the seat and put his arms around her. All the things he'd learned at the prenatal class about the stages of labour completely eluded him, but maybe Liz could tell him if he asked the questions calmly. 'How long have you been having the contractions? How close are they?'

'D-definite contractions for about an hour. But I think I've been in labour much longer.' She sniffed, wiping her cheeks with her hands, before she laid her head on his shoulder. 'They're about th-three minutes apart, maybe a bit shorter.'

He kissed her forehead. 'So what stage is that?'

'Early labour.'

'Okay. So the baby's still a little way off making her grand appearance?'

'Y-yes, I think so. And my waters haven't broken.'

'That's a good sign, isn't it?'

'Mmm-hmm.'

'I don't think we'll try to get up to Aunty Peg's now.' He pictured the control-room map in his head. Ernie Thomas's weekender was going to be their best bet.

'No. I had to turn back from both gullies. This is the highest point between them so I though it'd be safest here.'

'Good thinking.' He was proud of her resourcefulness.

'Except I skidded and the wheel ended up in the ditch.' She sounded tired, but then, 'Oh, my God.' She pushed away so she could look at him, her eyes fierce with accusation. 'How did you get here? Jack! You've come through Green Gully. You could have been killed.'

'Hey, I'm too ornery to let a little bit of water defeat me.' He gave her a quick smile. 'Come on. Let's get you over to the four-wheel drive. I know where we can go for shelter.'

He helped her out of the car and then, despite her protest, carried her over to his vehicle. With her settled on the back seat, he grabbed his sleeping bag and shook it out.

'What do we need from your car?' He tucked the bag around her. 'I'll get your medical bag. Anything else?'

'Aunty Peg's present. It's on the front seat. She's given us some nappies. We can use them for—for…' Her voice tailed off, her expression drawn.

'Sure. They'll come in handy.' He cupped her cheek and leaned over to give her a kiss. 'We can do this, Liz.'

'Yes.' The word was little more than a whisper.

'Just think of the stories you'll be able to tell your grandchildren.'

She gave him a wan smile. 'About how their granddaddy galloped through storms and flooded rivers to deliver their mother?'

'Yeah, those stories.' He grinned at her. 'Work on that image. I fancy being the hero of the hour. I'll be back in a flash.'

He walked across to her car, taking the opportunity to give himself a pep talk. He had to push his own fear back. Providing encouragement and support for the birth were the only things he could do for his wife. He was going to do them bloody well.

Back at his vehicle, he found Liz in the grip of another contraction. He dumped the gift and the box of produce on the front passenger seat and slid into the back beside her to wait out the pain.

When her breathing steadied and she opened her eyes again, he said, 'We'll head to Ernie Thomas's weekender. The turn-off is just around the corner.'

'Okay.'

Back in the front seat, he lifted the handpiece of the CB and turned to Liz. 'I'm going to call Danny and let him know what's happening.'

The unit gave a static crackle.

'Danny? I've found Liz. Over.'

'Copy that. How is she?'

He reached over and took her hand, giving it a quick squeeze as he held her eyes with his. Projecting all the confidence he could into his voice, he said, 'Next time you see us, we'll be parents.'

Just saying the words had a fresh wave of panic crashing over him. He fought the instinct to look away from Liz. Hell, he couldn't hide from her at this critical point. He had to do better. She had no choice but to have the baby now and his job was to help her. They were in this together.

Danny's raw oath ripped through the air, summing up Jack's feelings exactly. Then came a more moderate, 'Good luck.'

'Thanks.' He swallowed. *We'll need it.* But he didn't let the words escape. 'It's too risky for us to try to come back into town. Green Gully's getting pretty deep. Ernie's shack is close so that's where we're headed now. Can you put Tony Costello on standby up at the hospital in case we have any problems? Over.'

'Will do. I'll let the McLeods know you've found Liz, too. Peg's been on the phone.'

'Thanks, Danny.'

'Sarah sends her love. Me, too. Over and out.'

Jack signed off and hung up the handset. 'Set, gorgeous?'

'Yes.'

'Good girl.' He lifted her hand to his mouth, pressing his lips to her chilled fingers. 'It's not far.'

A few minutes later he turned into the concealed driveway and wound up a steep drive to brake in front of a ramshackle miner's hut. A chimney flue poked out of the rusted iron roof, promising the possibility of warmth within.

'Here we are, sweetheart. Home sweet home for the next few hours. I'll go and open up.'

'Won't it be locked?'

'Minor obstacle. I know where Ernie keeps a spare key.'

'Under the mat?' Liz murmured.

'How'd you guess?'

She rewarded him with a small chuckle. 'I know Ernie.'

Jack's breath steamed in the frosty air as he crossed the short distance to the hut. Dry wood was stacked to the eaves under the verandah, despite his past advice that it was a fire hazard. Thank goodness Ernie was a stubborn old beggar who didn't listen to well-meant advice from his local fire-brigade chief.

The air inside was a little musty, but the single room was tidy and a box of kindling stood beside the pot-belly. And he knew the steel cabinet always held a good supply of securely stored tinned food. He lit the gas lamp and trimmed the wick to provide a comfortable light. Then he found a foam mattress rolled up in a sealed box and laid it out on the bed.

Liz had her eyes closed when he went back to the car. 'Okay, darling, your palace awaits.'

She looped her arm around his neck as he scooped her off the seat, still bundled up warmly in the sleeping bag. She was so small and fragile. How on earth was she going to manage the task before her? He clenched his jaw, hugging her close as he carried her inside to put her on the bed.

Stepping back, he curled his hands into fists in an effort to dissipate his fear. 'Sweetheart, I'm going to get the fire going.'

'Okay.'

He could hear her breathing her way through another contraction as he brought in some wood and prepared a bed of kindling in the firebox. Soon the comforting crackle of burning logs filled the cabin.

'That should do it.' He dusted off his hands and turned to catch Liz watching him with dark, sombre eyes. He smiled with an assurance he was far from feeling. 'Okay, what can I get you? A cuppa? Warm compress?'

'Please. To both. With some sugar if Ernie has it.'

'Ernie has everything.' He set a billy full of water on the small portable gas stove. 'God bless him and his comfortable weekends away from Mrs T. in the bush.'

'Yes.' She sounded subdued. 'Jack, I'll need a mirror so I can check progress later.'

'Okay.' He walked to the door.

'Wh-where are you going? You're not going to leave me? Are you?' The panic-filled words tore his heart.

'Hey, darlin', no way.' He crossed to the bed in two strides and gathered her into his arms. 'I'm just going to be outside. All you need to do is yell if you need me. I want to get the rest of my kit while it's not raining and I'll check Ernie's bathroom for a mirror. Okay?'

'O-okay.' But her arms came around him and she hung on tightly for a long moment. When she pulled back slightly she managed a small smile, her eyes clinging to his through a veil of moisture. 'I guess there's no chance now of that epidural I was s-so adamant about *n-not* having, is there? Or a Caesarean.'

'Hey. You're not going to need them. You can do this.' He brushed her damp hair back from her face and kissed her forehead. 'We've been to all the classes and we know what to do, don't we? We're just going to take all the time we need to get this right.'

'But wh-what if I can't do it?'

'You can. You know you can, Liz.' He swallowed.

Another contraction hit her. She slid to kneel on the floor as the pain demanded her concentration for long seconds. He moved with her, holding her hands. Her fingernails dug sharply into his palms as she puffed. The discomfort gave him a tiny, welcome respite from his own anxiety.

When her breathing eased, she looked at him again, worry etched sharply into her features. 'What if you're right? What if the baby's too big? What if she's breech? What if she gets stuck? What if—?'

'Stop it, Liz. She won't get stuck,' said Jack decisively, as if willing it could make it so. Seeing her like this, so vulnerable, wrenched at him. She was always so in control, so capable. 'Remember what you told me. Remember what Julie said? Nature works these things out.'

Her eyes were black holes of fear and he could feel her trembling. He swallowed hard, grabbing for control, desperately searching for something to say that might help her.

'There's been no indication there would be a problem on any of your scans, has there?'

He waited until she shook her head. 'Your body's ready for this.'

She was relying on him to stay calm, but the truth of the matter was, he was terrified. He couldn't let it show. The birth was going to happen here and now. The only way he could help was by convincing Liz that they could do it. All of his misgivings about a natural delivery had to be put aside. He had no choice—*they* had no choice.

'I shouldn't have gone out today,' she moaned, her voice thick with unshed tears. 'Oh, God, what if I've put our daughter at risk by being so bloody-minded?'

'You haven't. Liz, you have to let go, let your body do the job. Trust yourself.'

Her eyes closed. Was she shutting him out?

God, if he couldn't convince her that she could deliver their daughter, he'd have failed her. If she didn't relax, she was in for an even more difficult time. What if she really couldn't do this? What if he lost her, lost them both? He couldn't let that happen. *Wouldn't* let that happen. But he'd never felt so powerless in his life.

'I trust you, darlin'.' His voice was hoarse with suppressed emotion. 'You can do this.'

CHAPTER SIXTEEN

IN THE subdued light of the cabin, moisture glistened along Liz's eyelashes. A fat tear gathered to roll down her cheek to the edge of her jaw.

If he could have, Jack would willingly have suffered the pain for her. But all he could do was give her support and encouragement. This agony wasn't his. It wasn't his body struggling to give birth. He hadn't fully understood how helpless he would feel.

How much longer could he be strong in the face of her fear? Even knowing how infectious someone else's terror could be wasn't helping him quash his own. But if he went under, he'd make her job that much harder.

He mustn't succumb.

A snippet from the prenatal class came back with sudden clarity. 'Remember what Julie said about the transition phase? How you'd feel as though everything was too much, too hard?' He held his breath as he waited for her response. 'Liz?'

Finally, she nodded.

'She said it'll pass. Remember?' *Soon. Let it be soon.* He listened to the deep, shuddering breath she took, prayed she would find the serenity to go on.

'Yes.' She inhaled again, held the air a moment then exhaled. When she opened her eyes again to look at him she seemed steadier. 'Yes. You're right. I remember.'

'I love you.'

She smiled tremulously. 'I love you, too.'

'You're an amazing and brave and beautiful woman, Mrs Campbell.' He lifted a hand to cup her cheek, ran his thumb across the soft skin. The changes that were taking place within her body even as he sat here with her had him in awe.

'Thank you.' She turned her lips to his palm. 'I…I don't know how I'd have coped if you weren't here.'

'You would have, sweetheart. But I'm glad I'm here, too.' He grinned at her. 'Besides, it's the least I could do since I'm partly responsible for getting you in this state in the first place.'

She didn't smile as he'd intended. Instead, her eyes filled and her chin wobbled.

'Jack, I'm sorry.' Her breath hitched as she looked down at her hands.

'Hey, what for?'

'F-for trapping you with this pregnancy.'

'Hell, darling, where did that come from? I thought we'd been through this.' He struggled to change gears to keep up with her.

'I—I know. I'm just s-so afraid you're going to end up hating me and our daughter.'

He lifted her chin so she looked at him directly. 'This is because of your visit with Patrice, isn't it?'

Her eyes clung to his, her anguish clear. 'Dad was forced to marry Mum because she got pregnant with me. Th-they made each other so miserable and bitter. I don't want that for us, for Emma.'

'I'm *not* the man your father was and you're not like your mother. I want you and I *want* our daughter.'

'D-do you?'

'Yes. How could I not, sweetheart? You're everything I need.'

After a moment, her tired face moved into a tentative smile.

'We're not going to make a mess of our marriage the way your parents did.' He gave her a quick kiss. 'Got it?'

'Got it.'

'Good.' He grinned. 'No more of this nonsense. We've got important things to do, okay?'

'O-okay.'

He looked over to where the billy was steaming. 'How about I make you that warm compress and something to drink?'

With hot and cold water mixed to a reasonable temperature, he wet a towel and wrung it out. Liz was still kneeling beside the bed. He helped her adjust her clothing so he could tuck the warm, damp pad against her lower back.

'That feels good.' She sighed as the heat seeped into her tired muscles. 'Thanks.'

Out of the corner of her eye she watched him walk back to the stove. A moment later he was back, pressing an enamel mug into her hand. He crouched beside her, his hand rubbing large circles across her back.

'Okay for a few minutes while I go out and get my kit, sweetheart?'

'Yes. I'm fine now.' As she spoke, she realised it was true.

Jack had given her that. He'd pulled her back from the edge of the panic that had threatened to tear her apart. He was so strong. His confidence in her warmed her, lifted her spirits. Made her really believe she could get through this with his help.

She watched the door close behind him. What had happened to her? Any medical student worth their salt knew panic and tension made pain worse. And hadn't she seen it time after time in the emergency department? Yet, in the grip of her own fright, she'd forgotten until Jack had reminded her of Julie's words. She smiled wryly. The learning curve of pregnancy was far steeper than she'd expected.

Her smile slipped. If Jack hadn't come to find her she'd have been alone with all her fears.

His love and determination had given her the reassurance she'd needed about their marriage, about their future. They weren't going to make the same mistakes her parents had—they could choose to be happy.

And he was right about this birth, too—she had to trust her body to do what it needed to. This time she couldn't use just her medical training, she had to use the unfamiliar tools of intuition and faith.

And right now her body was telling her she needed to move. She pushed herself to her feet as Jack came back into the cabin. A warm gush of liquid flowed down her thighs as she straightened up.

'Oh, blast!'

At her yelp he came instantly to her side, his face sharp with concern. 'What's wrong? Should you be standing?'

'My waters have just broken.'

She heard him swallow. 'So the baby's coming right now?'

'Not this very minute, but soon, I think.' She smiled at him, but he didn't return it.

'Let me help you sit. Should you lie down?' He tried to turn her back towards the bed.

'I'm fine, Jack.' She reached up to touch his face. 'Jack. Darling, I'm fine. I need to stand just now, maybe move around a bit.'

'Oh. Okay.' He ran a hand through his hair and suddenly looked a little lost. 'What can I do?'

'Help me change out of these wet clothes, please, darling.'

She looked down on his dark head as he bent to strip off her damp leggings then wipe the moisture from her legs with a towel. The tenderness of his intimate care melted her heart. She reached out and touched the exposed nape of his neck.

He looked up, his eyes meeting hers for a long, silent moment.

'Thank you for coming to find me.'

'I had to, Liz,' he said, rising to his feet and taking her in his arms, one hand resting on her belly. 'I knew you needed me.'

'I do need you. Always.' She rested her head on his shoulder, rejoicing in the strength and comfort hc gave her.

'I've got a flannelette shirt in my kit that'll keep you warm.'

After he'd helped her into the roomy garment, she rolled the sleeves up and tied the front ends together above her bulge.

'The latest in delivery-suite fashion.'

'You look stunning.'

'Oh, sure.'

'I've never meant anything more in my life, darling.' He kissed her hard. 'Okay, what's next?'

An hour and a half later Liz watched as Emma Elizabeth Campbell made her entrance into the world straight into Jack's strong, sure hands. He lifted the baby reverently to place her on Liz's stomach.

'She's beautiful.' His husky voice was filled with the same wonder that Liz felt.

'Yes, she is, isn't she?' She stroked her daughter's cheek, smiling when the baby turned her head, her little mouth making sucking motions. 'I think she's hungry.'

'I guess being born is hard work,' he said in hushed tones.

As she manoeuvred Emma's mouth to her nipple, Liz heard him draw in a sharp breath. She looked up to see his eyes glistening with moisture, his throat working. 'Darling? What's wrong?'

'I'm—I'm a dad.' When he met her gaze his was dark and intense. 'I want to be a *good* dad.'

She felt her throat close on a hot lump of emotion. After all Jack had done for her here today, the thought that he had any doubts about himself was intolerable. She could help him, that was her choice, her responsibility. To make sure he knew he was a welcome part of Emma's life always.

'You will be a good father, darling. You already are. The very best. Thanks to you, our daughter arrived safely.'

'That was you, sweetheart. You did an awesome job.'

'*We* did an awesome job here today. I couldn't have done it without your support. You never faltered, never thought we couldn't do it.'

His eyes slid away from hers guiltily.

She laughed softly, the urge to cry receding slightly. 'Well, you never let me *see* your doubts. You were strong when I needed you to be and that takes courage. You gave me the confidence to believe I could do this. We're a great team.'

'We are, aren't we?' He gave her his gorgeous cocky grin. 'I love you.'

'And I love you, Jack Campbell. Emma's very lucky to have you.' She smiled at him through fresh tears in her eyes. 'And so am I.'

Jack's lips came down to claim hers in a tender caress.

MILLS & BOON

AUGUST 2009 HARDBACK TITLES

ROMANCE

Desert Prince, Bride of Innocence	Lynne Graham
Raffaele: Taming His Tempestuous Virgin	Sandra Marton
The Italian Billionaire's Secretary Mistress	Sharon Kendrick
Bride, Bought and Paid For	Helen Bianchin
Hired for the Boss's Bedroom	Cathy Williams
The Christmas Love-Child	Jennie Lucas
Mistress to the Merciless Millionaire	Abby Green
Italian Boss, Proud Miss Prim	Susan Stephens
Proud Revenge, Passionate Wedlock	Janette Kenny
The Buenos Aires Marriage Deal	Maggie Cox
Betrothed: To the People's Prince	Marion Lennox
The Bridesmaid's Baby	Barbara Hannay
The Greek's Long-Lost Son	Rebecca Winters
His Housekeeper Bride	Melissa James
A Princess for Christmas	Shirley Jump
The Frenchman's Plain-Jane Project	Myrna Mackenzie
Italian Doctor, Dream Proposal	Margaret McDonagh
Marriage Reunited: Baby on the Way	Sharon Archer

HISTORICAL

The Brigadier's Daughter	Catherine March
The Wicked Baron	Sarah Mallory
His Runaway Maiden	June Francis

MEDICAL™

Wanted: A Father for her Twins	Emily Forbes
Bride on the Children's Ward	Lucy Clark
The Rebel of Penhally Bay	Caroline Anderson
Marrying the Playboy Doctor	Laura Iding

0709 Gen Std LP

MILLS & BOON

AUGUST 2009 LARGE PRINT TITLES

ROMANCE

The Spanish Billionaire's Pregnant Wife	Lynne Graham
The Italian's Ruthless Marriage Command	Helen Bianchin
The Brunelli Baby Bargain	Kim Lawrence
The French Tycoon's Pregnant Mistress	Abby Green
Diamond in the Rough	Diana Palmer
Secret Baby, Surprise Parents	Liz Fielding
The Rebel King	Melissa James
Nine-to-Five Bride	Jennie Adams

HISTORICAL

The Disgraceful Mr Ravenhurst	Louise Allen
The Duke's Cinderella Bride	Carole Mortimer
Impoverished Miss, Convenient Wife	Michelle Styles

MEDICAL™

Children's Doctor, Society Bride	Joanna Neil
The Heart Surgeon's Baby Surprise	Meredith Webber
A Wife for the Baby Doctor	Josie Metcalfe
The Royal Doctor's Bride	Jessica Matthews
Outback Doctor, English Bride	Leah Martyn
Surgeon Boss, Surprise Dad	Janice Lynn

ROMANCE

A Bride for His Majesty's Pleasure	Penny Jordan
The Master Player	Emma Darcy
The Infamous Italian's Secret Baby	Carole Mortimer
The Millionaire's Christmas Wife	Helen Brooks
Duty, Desire and the Desert King	Jane Porter
Royal Love-Child, Forbidden Marriage	Kate Hewitt
One-Night Mistress...Convenient Wife	Anne McAllister
Prince of Montéz, Pregnant Mistress	Sabrina Philips
The Count of Castelfino	Christina Hollis
Beauty and the Billionaire	Barbara Dunlop
Crowned: The Palace Nanny	Marion Lennox
Christmas Angel for the Billionaire	Liz Fielding
Under the Boss's Mistletoe	Jessica Hart
Jingle-Bell Baby	Linda Goodnight
The Magic of a Family Christmas	Susan Meier
Mistletoe & Marriage	Patricia Thayer & Donna Alward
Her Baby Out of the Blue	Alison Roberts
A Doctor, A Nurse: A Christmas Baby	Amy Andrews

HISTORICAL

Devilish Lord, Mysterious Miss	Annie Burrows
To Kiss a Count	Amanda McCabe
The Earl and the Governess	Sarah Elliott

MEDICAL™

Country Midwife, Christmas Bride	Abigail Gordon
Greek Doctor: One Magical Christmas	Meredith Webber
Spanish Doctor, Pregnant Midwife	Anne Fraser
Expecting a Christmas Miracle	Laura Iding

0809 Gen Std LP

MILLS & BOON

SEPTEMBER 2009 LARGE PRINT TITLES

ROMANCE

The Sicilian Boss's Mistress — Penny Jordan
Pregnant with the Billionaire's Baby — Carole Mortimer
The Venadicci Marriage Vengeance — Melanie Milburne
The Ruthless Billionaire's Virgin — Susan Stephens
Italian Tycoon, Secret Son — Lucy Gordon
Adopted: Family in a Million — Barbara McMahon
The Billionaire's Baby — Nicola Marsh
Blind-Date Baby — Fiona Harper

HISTORICAL

Lord Braybrook's Penniless Bride — Elizabeth Rolls
A Country Miss in Hanover Square — Anne Herries
Chosen for the Marriage Bed — Anne O'Brien

MEDICAL™

The Children's Doctor's Special Proposal — Kate Hardy
English Doctor, Italian Bride — Carol Marinelli
The Doctor's Baby Bombshell — Jennifer Taylor
Emergency: Single Dad, Mother Needed — Laura Iding
The Doctor Claims His Bride — Fiona Lowe
Assignment: Baby — Lynne Marshall